HER SENSUAL PROTECTOR

NIGHT STORM, BOOK FIVE

CAITLYN O'LEARY

Dedication

To the men and women who serve, and the people who love them.

SYNOPSIS

The first time Navy SEAL, Leo Perez sees Daisy Squires, he is stopped in his tracks. There she was, slamming her fists on the table, making six men jump to attention in the Afghanistan embassy. It was a beautiful sight to behold. Somebody better find her kidnapped father, and fast.

At her wits' end, Daisy realized she would have to rely on the special forces team to rescue her father, which killed her; shouldn't she be doing something—*anything*— to help facilitate her father's safe return? But when Leo Perez told her to trust him, she started to believe. Maybe trust was finally an option for her.

Daisy and Leo soon find themselves immersed in a situation they never thought possible as terrorist forces gain strength. Will their emerging love be strong enough to face the deadly forces determined to stop Daisy?

1

LEO WISHED HIS BOSS HAD SENT SOMEONE ELSE, ANYBODY else, but Max had raised his eyebrow and sent him. Deep down, or not that deep down, Leo knew why. But it still rankled. Fine, he had a way with the ladies, but this was a mission, for God's sake. This was a fucking mission in Afghanistan, not the time or place for the charm offensive.

But when he saw just how poorly the diplomats and phony diplomats were doing, he could see where charm could be really useful. Just how dumb were these guys? Even the CIA plants had their heads firmly embedded up their asses.

"Ms. Squires, your presence here, and the media storm your family and friends have created in the United States, is detrimental to us finding and safely returning your father," the US Ambassador to Afghanistan said to the petite woman sitting in the chair across from his at the conference room table. This was the fourth time he'd said something like that to her. Leo could tell she was getting hot under the collar.

"What else would you have me do? Other people have been kidnapped in Afghanistan and you have done nothing. Nothing has been done for that reporter, Dick Summers." Her tone was savage.

Ooops, the gloves have come off. Leo smothered a grin.

"That's not true," the ambassador said.

"Oh really," she said sarcastically. "Obviously nothing of note, since he's been missing for four months, and you still haven't managed his release."

One of the lower-level diplomatic aides standing behind the ambassador spoke up. "We're working on his release, as well as your father's. Now, your dad has only been missing for a week. Nobody understands why he decided to come to Afghanistan when the rest of his team was still in Pakistan. It is our understanding that is where the polio inoculations are needed, not here in Afghanistan." The aide seemed nice enough. But not so nice when you considered he was one of five men who were standing beside the ambassador, all leaning over the conference room table, clearly trying to intimidate the petite woman.

"Just contact Dr. Williams in Pakistan, you'll find that they traced cases of polio to villages here in Afghanistan. My father and Dr. Williams decided my father would be the best one to come over here since he spoke Dari. He crossed the border legally, there wasn't anything secretive about his arrival."

Leo admired Daisy Squires' fierceness when surrounded by all the men intent on poking holes in her story. Her will was indomitable. Leo casually leaned back against the far wall, well away from the action. He made it clear he was just observing. What's more, the fact that they were all in suits and he was wearing fatigues should have made it even more obvious.

Another man glared down at Daisy. "Ten years ago your father was in Palestine, and he was working with Hamas. He has a penchant for working for terrorist organizations, isn't that true?" His voice sliced through the room.

Leo continued to keep his casual stance but made sure he could catch every word of the conversation.

"You obviously have faulty records," she said scornfully. "You need to talk to the Palestine Unit in our embassy in Israel. That was all cleared up back then. My father does *not* work with terrorist organizations. He cares for sick and wounded children. Full stop."

The same oily dirtbag continued his interrogation. "I have checked with the Ambassador there, and the records are vague."

"That's on the State Department, now isn't it?" She stood up and placed her hands on the table, leaning forward. "I strongly suggest you find someone who worked there at the time. In the meantime, find my father. He's. Been. Kidnapped."

"Ms. Squires, it's not that easy." The ambassador tried to soothe her.

She slapped the table. "Then make it that easy. I got this meeting because of the stink my family is making in the U.S. That's nothing compared to what they're prepared to do. Wait until the petitions and the viral social media campaigns begin."

"Ms. Squires, you need to settle down." It was the man who had accused her father of working with terrorists. "You have no idea what we have to deal with daily, and the type of situation your dad is in. You need to leave it to us to handle, and go back to the States."

Come on Daisy, let him have it. If he could, Leo would have rubbed his hands together.

"I'm not leaving Afghanistan without my father. You're stuck with me. As to not understanding how things work? You're wrong. I run W.A.N.T., Women Acting Now and Tomorrow. I know exactly what your situation is."

One of the men snorted. She turned her head to face him.

"My charity works in Nigeria. You know, the country that is home to Boko Haram? I'm well aware that here you're dealing with Al-Qaeda or the Haqqani Network, but good news, my father has been gone for a little less than a week. You *can* find him. You *can* get this done."

She was magnificent. Leo smothered a grin as he watched her make mincemeat out of the ambassador and his five flunkies.

"We don't negotiate with terrorists," the dick diplomat said.

He's such an asshole, I'm about ready to take him out back.

"I'm not asking you to," Daisy said with disgust. "You go to the Afghan government and have them talk to the Taliban, or you talk directly with the Taliban, who then talks to those two terrorist organizations."

She was exactly right, that's how it worked. God, he was loving this. The suits were about ready to piss their pants.

Daisy reached for her leather backpack. "I will be back in twenty-four hours. I expect an update on your progress." She walked around the conference room table. If she hadn't been wearing heels, Leo didn't think she'd be even five-feet tall. But that hadn't stopped her from taking down a roomful of diplomats and CIA professionals. As she passed by Leo she winked at him, then walked out the glass door.

WHAT IN THE hell was her oldest brother up to? He must have ruffled a whole hell of a lot of feathers stateside since she'd arrived in Kabul this morning, if the ambassador and five flunkies met with her. She'd tagged two as CIA, the rest as mid-level diplomatic aides, and one who gave her hope. They wouldn't have had a casual military guy in there unless he was listening in for potential intelligence for some kind of op.

The sun blinded her when she strode out of the embassy. She stopped for just a moment to take off the linen jacket she'd been wearing and put on her Oakley sunglasses. One of the few things she splurged on, but oh so necessary when she was in countries like Afghanistan where the sun practically touched the ground.

Her driver was still waiting for her.

"Malek, take me to the hotel. There will be people following us, but don't worry," Daisy told her driver in perfectly enunciated Dari, the national language of Afghanistan.

"Should we be worried?" Her driver was nothing if not pragmatic.

"They will be members of the embassy. They are harmless."

"Americans following Americans," he coughed out a laugh. "This is something new."

They were soon at the Kabul Serena Hotel, and Malek stopped and showed his ID. He was let through the gate, then security used a mirror on a stick to check the underside of their car for bombs before letting them drive to the front of the hotel.

Daisy knew not to even bother opening the door of the backseat because there would be somebody opening it for her. And there was. She shrugged on her jacket and took off her sunglasses as she walked into the air-conditioned hotel lobby. Her stride didn't vary when she spotted the same soldier who had been loitering in the back of the conference room, seated in the lobby waiting for her.

How in the hell did he make it here so fast?

When he saw her coming his way, he stood up and smiled. It was a genuine smile, unlike all the others she'd been subjected to at the embassy.

"Who are you?" she asked as she took his outstretched hand and shook it.

"Chief Petty Officer, Leo Perez, at your service."

"Navy, huh? You wouldn't be a member of the acclaimed Navy SEALs would you?"

"Now ma'am, what could possibly make you ask such a question?" his smile was bright against his brown skin.

Daisy smiled back.

"Call it a lucky hunch."

"Ms. Squires, based on everything I know about you, I don't think much comes down to luck. I think that you get things done through determination, intelligence, and hard work."

"Ah, someone smart enough to have looked me up. I'm impressed."

"Why don't we have a drink in the restaurant so we're not quite so conspicuous?"

"That's probably a good idea," she admitted. Even though she didn't want to be, she was flattered. There was something about having this man think highly of her that warmed her.

They walked across the lobby to the upscale restaurant and were quickly seated. Daisy noted that Leo's Dari was almost as fluent as her own. She should have expected this. She had dealt with special forces in the past when she was in Nigeria. These men were extremely smart and capable; only a fool would underestimate them.

"You have a question?" Leo asked after they had both ordered some chai tea.

"Not a question, just an observation. You speak Dari extremely well. Very few Americans do."

"The lady next door who babysat me while my mom worked was Persian. Farsi was easy enough to pick up. Then when I did some work over here in Afghanistan, I worked on the Dari dialect of Farsi."

Their waiter tea set in front of them. Leo made small talk with him.

"Yep, you make it sound easy," Daisy said in English.

Leo tilted his head and his eyes narrowed. "Yet you speak four different languages, don't you?"

"Four fluently, a couple more where I can get by. It's necessary when I travel so much for my job." She smiled in response. Then she took a cup of the *very* sweet tea. She had missed this when she was in America. She watched as Leo winced.

"Not to your taste?" she grinned.

"I can't get used to the fact that they dump a cup of sugar in the tea."

"The more sugar, the more honor they're bestowing on

you. If they didn't like you, you wouldn't get any." The hot beverage was making her warm, so she took off her jacket. "So how did you get to my hotel so fast?"

"Motorcycle. That way I could weave in and out of traffic."

She nodded, it made sense. "You must not value your life, or have a daredevil gene. You could have gotten killed out there."

Leo laughed. The sound ricocheted through her body, bringing senses alive that she hadn't felt in a long time. Daisy couldn't help but smile with him.

"Ms. Squires, that was just an appetizer of what my normal day is like. Would you have come down from your room to meet me if I'd arrived after you?"

"Yes."

Leo's eyes widened just a little. "Huh, what do you know? I believe you."

"Everyone should. I don't lie. If someone had bothered to ask me something relevant I would have told them the truth."

They both took sips of their tea as they considered one another.

"So, what *is* relevant to your father's kidnapping?"

"Like usual, he's managed to piss off just about everybody he shouldn't. He pissed off Dr. Williams so much that he sent him packing to Afghanistan."

"Why?"

"Most people think polio has been eradicated worldwide. It hasn't been. It's still endemic in Pakistan and Afghanistan."

"Endemic?" Leo asked. "I'm pretty sure I know what the word means, but define it for me, just to make sure I'm clear."

"It denotes an area where a disease is commonly found. It's a tribute to the hard work of dedicated men and women that it's been clamped down in almost every other country. This is where people are likely to have and spread it, while other places might get it from unsanitary water. Therefore Dr. Williams and his team were working to vaccinate the final couple of villages in Pakistan and then they were going to move to Afghanistan. They were running into the regular obstacles, but with the right kind of diplomacy, they could have worked through it. Of course, my father went behind people's backs and stirred up the cleric elders. It was a mess."

"The imams? What did he do?" Leo asked.

"He went to the kids' schools and vaccinated them, totally against the wishes of their parents. It was unacceptable. But if you ask my father, he was doing the right thing. Dr. Williams was working with the women in the village whose children had gotten sick with polio. His campaign was working, but oh no, my father just had to stomp all over their beliefs."

Leo took another sip of his tea. "You sound very angry."

"Only because I am. This is my father's way of doing things. It would be one thing if it only put himself in danger, but it puts everyone around him in danger, too. Don't get me wrong, I think what he's doing is noble work, trying to make sure kids stay healthy, but he still could have gotten that done without putting himself and all the rest of the doctors' and nurses' lives in jeopardy. That's what he does, he just forges ahead, damn the consequences."

Leo gave her an intent look. "Did you and your family ever go with him? Did it put you in danger?"

Her next sip of the sweet tea almost made her gag; suddenly it was *too* sweet as her mind filled with memories. "Yes."

"Yes to both questions?" he asked gently.

She nodded.

"That must have been hard for you growing up."

"Not really. My mother divorced him when I was four years old. By the time I was six my mom had married Alistair Barret. For all intents and purposes, he's my dad."

Leo nodded.

Daisy might not ever lie, but she didn't like the way Leo seemed to read between the lines of her story. Most people didn't ask such pertinent questions. It made her uneasy.

Leo looked down at his phone for a moment, then back up at her "You have two brothers and a sister. Do they consider Ambassador Barret to be their father as well?"

Daisy had her first real laugh of the day.

"They're ten, twelve, and fifteen years older than me. They weren't as lucky as I was. They grew up with our father, so no, they don't consider Alistair their father, which is unfortunate. As far as I'm concerned they got the booby-prize, after what Ethan Squires put them through."

Leo winced. "You don't pull any of your punches, do you?"

Daisy shrugged. "They each have their own story to tell, and so does my mother. And I have mine. When you combine them all, I don't think my conclusion is that far out of reach."

"So if you're not a fan of your biological dad, why are you here rattling cages?"

"Because I love my siblings and they want our father rescued. I might not like him, but I certainly don't wish him dead. So my family and I agreed that I was the best one to send. Rattling cages is something I excel at."

2

LEO'S LIPS TWITCHED. THE WAY SHE TALKED, HE DIDN'T doubt it. Still, she might have taken on the dweebs in the embassy, but what she didn't know is that her quasi-father had been kidnapped by the Haqqani Network, and it didn't get any uglier than that.

She raised one eyebrow. "Handsome, I see the wheels turning. Anything you want to share with me?"

"You think I'm handsome?"

"I told you I don't lie. You're hot. Somehow I can't help but wonder if that was taken into consideration when they knew you would be dealing with a woman."

"A smart, beautiful woman who rattles cages and speaks Dari. Quite the combo kit, Ms. Squires, or can I call you Daisy?"

"I think since I just said you were hot, calling me Daisy would be appropriate at this point," she laughed. "But I must say, you do lay it on a bit thick."

He took a slow sip of tea and she watched him. "I just call it as I see it. I'm taking a page out of your book, no lying."

"No lying sounds good, really good." She put both hands around her teacup. "Tell me how you fit into the picture. I'm assuming you're here to assess whether my father can be rescued. Am I right?"

"Something like that."

"Hey, you just promised not to tell any lies," she complained.

The waiter came and poured more tea into their cups for the second time.

"At this rate, I'm going to float out of here," Leo complained.

"The rule is, you have to turn over your cup, or they'll keep filling it."

"How am I ever going to get to do that, they don't give me a chance to empty it?"

"My advice is that you drink faster."

Leo knew she was laughing at him.

"Leo, what's your assessment? What are you going to tell your superiors? Is a rescue possible?"

"Yes."

"Then why no rescue for the reporter?"

"I don't know for sure."

"Can you take some guesses?"

"Not my place."

"For someone who wasn't going to tell me any lies, you're not very forthcoming."

"But, I haven't lied to you." He watched to see if she would see the difference.

She picked up her teacup and smiled. "Good to know. So you'll answer what questions you can, and pass on the questions you can't, is that it?"

Leo nodded.

"I see you're not drinking your tea," she said as she nodded toward his cup.

"I figured out a third option. If I just leave it full, they can't pour more into my cup."

She grinned. "You're right." She took a long sip of her tea, then turned her cup over. "Are you hungry?" she asked.

"Always." Anytime he had a chance to eat something other than an MRE, he was in.

"A meal or a snack?" she asked.

Leo considered. He still had to report back to Max and meet with the team. "Have you had lunch yet?"

Daisy shook her head.

"Let's order food." He lifted his hand and the waiter came over. "Can you bring menus?" Leo asked in Dari. The waiter nodded and immediately came back with menus. He explained the specials in English.

Leo went with the cinnamon lamb kebabs and Daisy chose the eggplant dish. The waiter said he would be back out with some spicy chickpeas to start.

"You grew up in an embassy, huh?" Leo said. "What was that like?"

"Mom married Alistair when I was six, and he was the ambassador to Tajikistan at that point. His appointment lasted for twelve years."

"No wonder you're so comfortable with the Dari language. Tajikistan's national language is Tajik, so learning Dari was pretty easy, huh?"

"Exactly. I learned Russian while I lived there too. When I went to the International School, everything was in English but Tajik and Russian were the two compulsory second languages."

"Do all of your siblings speak as many different languages?" Leo asked.

"Pretty much. My older siblings spent a lot of time with my parents in Africa while the esteemed doctor was chasing everything from HIV to Ebola. They speak a lot of different African languages, while I grew up speaking more Middle Eastern languages."

Leo heard the bitterness in her voice, but her countenance didn't seem ready to share, so he didn't ask about it. Instead, he decided to stay on safer topics.

"But you do speak African languages according to your file."

Daisy grinned as she grabbed some chickpeas. "That must be one hell of a dossier you have on me. It couldn't have been the CIA who put it together, otherwise, the two CIA guys in the embassy would have known who I was. I didn't realize that special forces were investigators."

Leo smiled and helped himself to some chickpeas, happy that they had brought a bottle of mineral water to go with it. Spicy, crunchy nuts and sweet tea together sounded awful. He poured the water into both of their glasses.

"Yep, they definitely pegged you right in that thick dossier when they said you were smart. Which guys did you have figured as CIA?"

"There was the prick who kept trying to bully me. He was playing bad cop. I'd say this was his first field assignment. Then there was the one in the blue suit who didn't say a word, but he winced when the dumbass snarled at me. He must have been his superior. I'd say dick-boy is going to get an earful today."

Leo let out a laugh. "Yep, that's how I read it too. The blue suit is Tom Ludlum; he's a good guy. I would be surprised if he doesn't send that young guy back to the States. I don't think he's salvageable." Leo stopped talking as the waiter set down their food in front of them. It looked fantastic and smelled even better.

Daisy smirked.

"What?" Leo asked.

"Mine's better than yours. Check it out, I got a side of braised pumpkin with yogurt."

Leo looked. "You might be right. Are you a vegetarian?"

"Nope, just in the mood for eggplant." She started in on her food, and Leo followed suit. It gave him a chance to figure out what he wanted to ask next. He needed to find out exactly why Dr. Squires might have been targeted by the Haqqani Network. Any additional information he and his team could find out would really help before starting a mission to get him the hell out of their hands.

"You're looking at me funny," she said as she started in on the pumpkin side dish. "Just spit out whatever you have to say."

"Can you think of anything that your dad might have been doing besides inoculating children for polio, that might have pissed off the Haqqani Network?"

Daisy set down her fork and pressed her napkin against her clean lips. "My father could have done damn near anything. Let's begin with all the stupid moves he made in Pakistan. Dr. Williams was incensed that he had put their entire project in danger by his foolhardy moves. Seriously, polio is this close," she put her thumb and forefinger together up to her face. "This close to being eradicated in Pakistan and Afghanistan. These are the last two countries where it is endemic. Until men and women like Dr. Williams, and all of the local villagers who are working with him, can disrupt the transmission of this virus in Pakistan and Afghanistan, all other countries are at risk of importing polio into their country, especially those countries that are vulnerable."

"Which ones are vulnerable?"

"Those with poor immunization plans or poor health and public services. This is vitally important. And Ethan Squires is letting his impatience put it all at risk. He never cares about long-term repercussions. He just plows ahead, because his ego demands an immediate reward."

Leo heard the bitterness in her voice. It sounded deeply personal and filled with pain. What had her dad done to her to deserve those thoughts from such a compassionate woman?

"So he's done this before?"

"Oh yeah, he has. It doesn't matter whose life he puts at risk, as long as he gets that adrenaline high of being the medical God of the moment."

"Who else has he harmed?" Leo asked gently.

"You name it. The great doctor dragged our family to Swaziland in 1991 to help combat the measles outbreak. This was when the vaccines were available, but cases were surging. My mom didn't want to go. But she was young and tired, and really didn't know just how dangerous it was. He took them into the thick of things. Karen was ten and Brian was eight when they both contracted the disease. Karen almost died, and Brian was left sterile. To this day I don't know why she stayed with him after that."

"But she did, because you're here," Leo nodded to her to keep eating. She moved some of her food around on her plate.

"Yes, she did," Daisy admitted reluctantly. "I was a surprise baby. After the measles outbreak, Mom mostly stayed in the States, but she agreed one last time to go overseas. She said my father guilted her into it because he hadn't had a chance to spend much time with me. He promised it would be safe." Her voice trailed off.

Leo saw how her fist clenched on the table and he wanted to console her, but it wasn't his place.

"Was it safe?" Leo asked after the waiter left.

She shook her head. "This time it wasn't a disease. Mom got pregnant again. We were in the Brazilian rain forest. He had left us in a village that only spoke Portuguese, Mom and I didn't. She ended up having a miscarriage. I remember her crying in pain and me trying to give her food and water, trying to fix her, but she was too delirious to take in food or water. I kept kissing her forehead like she always did to me when I was sick, thinking that was something that would make her better, but it didn't. Finally, I went to the neighbors next door begging for help. They didn't understand me. There was no ambulance, nothing like that. A woman came to help Mom. They took me away from her," her hand dropped from the table to clutch her stomach. "It seemed like forever that I was at the neighbor's house. I thought she was dead. When my father eventually found me, I was inconsolable. He didn't tell me anything, he just left me at the neighbors for a long time, until finally, he brought me to see my mom." She rested her fist back up on the table.

"How old were you?"

"Four."

Leo pictured everything in vivid detail. The idea of Daisy, practically a baby, going through that horror, made his blood boil. How could a real man have done that to his wife and child?

This time when he saw the knuckles on her fist turn

bone-white he couldn't help himself, he reached out and put his hand over hers, his thumb smoothing across her taut knuckles.

She looked up at him, her expression confused. What? Was she not used to being touched by a man?

"Leo?" she began.

"What happened then?"

Her breath shuddered.

"Mom didn't look like Mom. She was so thin and gray. I wasn't allowed to hug her, and she kept crying a lot. I remember being so scared. Mom ended up lying down in the backseat of the jeep on the drive out of the jungle. Usually, I sat on her lap, but I wasn't allowed to do that either. My father tried to get me to sit on his lap up front, but I screamed and pulled away from him. I did everything possible to stay with my mom. He had to let me stay in the back, and I sat on the floorboards of the backseat. I got to hold her hand, even when she was asleep. On the entire two-day drive it seemed like I never slept once. I know that can't be true, but even thinking back on that time as an adult, I think it *was* true, ya know?"

God, it was so heartbreaking. He nodded at her, willing her to continue. When she didn't, he asked another question.

"What happened when you got out of the jungle?"

"Dad got Mom to a real hospital. This time I didn't have a choice but to be separated from her. Again, I thought she was dead. But I didn't cry, I didn't make a scene. I just let myself be taken away from the big white building and accompanied my father to some room he had rented. I never talked. I remember him trying to make me eat, but I refused. He must have talked to me. He must have tried to get through to me that Mom was okay and in a hospital to get better, but nothing penetrated—in my four-year-old brain she was dead and gone. I was in shock. I wouldn't eat, I wouldn't talk, I wasn't present."

"How long did that last?"

Big hazel eyes looked up at him. "I don't know. I never asked that question as I grew up. It seemed like forever as a child. But one day my father forced me into a car and we went back to the big white building that had eaten my mother. She came back out. I couldn't wrap my head around it. She looked like my mother again, but I wasn't the same little girl. I didn't talk. I didn't cry. I just clung to her. It was that way on the entire flight back to the United States. Finally, we got to my grandparent's house and everything was better."

She gave a false smile. "See? Happily ever after."

Leo snorted. "I can just see the traumatized baby that you were."

She pulled her hand away and put it into her lap, foregoing the food on her plate.

"Really, it was fine after that."

Leo nodded to her water. "Take a sip, you need it. As for the fact that you were fine after that, if that's what you need me to believe, then I'll believe it."

He nudged her water glass closer to her.

"You're kind of bossy."

He threw back his head and laughed. "I believe you were the one who slapped the table at six men in a conference room and told them to get their shit together. I'm a pussycat."

"Yes I did, so what are you going to do about rescuing my father?"

"We're doing it. Right now, my team is doing

reconnaissance. There are a lot of facets to this operation. Me getting information from you is just one angle. They're going to ping me when they have more news. In the meantime, I'm going to continue to ask you questions."

"Like what?"

"Like how you had the gumption to stand up to all of those men. I gotta tell you, you made quite a picture slapping that table. You say I'm bossy? Well compared to you, I'm a pussycat."

Daisy's lip lifted. "I might could remember doing that," she said as she picked up her water glass.

"Might could? I recognize that turn of phrase. What part of the South did you call home in the States?"

"My mom's dad worked for the state department. He and grandma have a big house in Ashburn Virginia. That's where Brian and Karen had been staying while Mom and I were in the jungle. Jim was already attending college at Georgetown University.

"When Grandpa Eddie found out about everything that happened in Brazil, he went ballistic. At least that's what Karen told me. I wasn't there when it happened. He didn't allow my father to stay at the family house. He closed ranks around Mom and us kids. Apparently, he hired the best lawyer in D.C. for his youngest daughter, and had the marriage dissolved in less than two months."

"I'd like your grandfather," Leo said with a smile.

"Just so long as you never got on his bad side," Daisy nodded.

3

"I'M SURPRISED THAT AFTER EVERYTHING YOUR MOTHER went through, she would be willing to get married again, especially so soon after the divorce."

"So was she." Daisy was eating her food again. She had a sparkle in her eye. "Alistair was everything my father wasn't. She met him when he came to visit Granddad at the house. He had been working for him at a mid-level cabinet post when he met my mom. According to Alistair, it was love at first sight. He put my mother and me first in all things. We were treated like the sun and moon in his universe. He hadn't been angling for an ambassadorship. When he got selected to run the Tajikistan embassy he was ready to turn it down. It was Mom who had to talk him into taking the post. She was convinced he could do great things. And he did."

"I saw that you went over there. Didn't you stay until you were sixteen?"

Daisy nodded.

"And your siblings?"

"They stayed back home. By that time Karen was

going to NYU, and Brian was immersed in high school and didn't want to leave. So he stayed with my grandparents."

"So it was just the three of you in Tajikistan?"

She nodded. "I went to the International School. I loved it there. Every day I learned something different, and I'm not talking about school, I'm talking about the country and culture. Not to mention all the things I learned living at the embassy."

"Like what?"

"Since I was so young when I arrived, nobody paid any attention to me, so I was in and out of Alistair's office all the time. As long as I was quiet and out of the way, it was amazing how many meetings I got to attend. I was small for my age, so that lasted until I began to develop. Up until that time, most people thought I was seven years old at the most."

"Really? The other diplomats really put up with that?"

"Not everyone. The autocratic countries were paranoid, but most Western countries didn't give it a second thought, unless there were delicate topics being discussed."

"No wonder you can handle your charity at such a young age. It must have been child's play. Most people in your position would have a master's degree or Ph.D., but you haven't even graduated college."

"Nope. The idea of sitting in class and being lectured to was my idea of hell. That was the reason touring the world when I graduated from the International School appealed to me."

"There were months and months that are unaccounted for during your tour. It's bugging the hell out of our communications guy," Leo laughed.

"What are you talking about? He could track me by my passport."

"Sure, you entered India in April 2015 and eleven months later you showed up in Nepal. Kane's still trying to figure out where you were during all that time in India."

Daisy's shoulders finally relaxed. She forked a bigger piece of her eggplant and ate it with relish. "It was a tough situation in India, but at least I could help."

"So where were you?"

"I spent most of my time in the state of Bangladesh. There was bad flooding. I helped where I could."

"That's all you're going to give me? Come on, give me more, I want to show up Kane. Please," Leo wheedled.

Daisy laughed. "Are you and your team members competitive?

"Honey, competitive doesn't even come close to covering it. Except when we're in the field working together, everything is a competition."

"Yeah, that's the way it is with my brothers. Jim was never into contact sports because his goal was to be a surgeon. Eventually, that changed. He's a brilliant scientist and works with a team to come up with different cutting-edge molecular and DNA sequencing that go into cures for some of the most virulent diseases known to mankind. But he still has a thing about hurting his hands. Meanwhile, Brian was into any sport that had a ball or a puck. They settled on golf. If I have to hear about one more round of golf, shot by fricking shot, I think I might put a bullet in one of their heads."

"Who wins most often?"

"It totally depends on the time of year. Brian runs one of the biggest accounting firms in Richmond. If it's near tax season he loses every time. Since Jim's a surgeon, he's constantly under pressure so he thrives on golf."

"What about your sister? Is she competitive?"

"Absolutely not. You couldn't get more laid back than Karen. She has three kids. She's the quintessential soccer mom—totally supportive, tries to get them to eat well, but she's not regimented about it. Her house is where all the other kids come to hang out. She met her husband in college and they still get caught by their kids making out on the sofa. I know because her fifteen-year-old daughter called and told me that she's traumatized for life."

"Traumatized? Just what were they doing?" Leo asked.

"According to Leah, it was everything. According to Karen, they had on all of their clothes. Paul's not talking. I figure it's something in between."

They both started laughing.

"That's quite the family you have," Leo grinned. "So who's in charge of making the stink back in the States?"

"It's June, so that'd be Brian. Alistair is helping. All three of my siblings are distraught. Even Mom is. That's the only reason I'm over here."

"I would have thought Alistair would have been the better choice," Leo probed.

"He's having some medical issues right now. Where possible, he's giving advice and counsel and family and friends are running with it."

Once again, Leo saw her tensing up. "Is he okay?"

She gave a sharp nod. She wasn't going to tell him anything else.

"Are you going to tell me anything more about the rescue plans for my father?"

"Right now we're still intelligence gathering. I needed to find out what possible reason the Haqqani Network would have to kidnap your father; that was the reason for me being at the embassy, and our lunch."

"Did you learn anything?"

"It sounds like your dad could have done myriad things to piss off some locals and made him a target for Islamic terrorists."

"Yep," Daisy said as she pushed her plate away. "That's Ethan Squires for you, always available to piss somebody off. Be it a four-year-old or an international network of terrorists, he's your man."

"Can I ask you a personal question?" Leo's voice was gentle.

"Have at it. I've told you things that most of the people who've known me for the last five years don't know."

"If you dislike your father so much, why are you here rattling cages?"

Daisy grimaced, but then her expression smoothed out. She would win an award at compartmentalizing. "Like I told you before, it's mostly for my siblings and the fact that I can't let him be hurt. I love my siblings. I still can't believe just how attached they are to him. I don't get it. Personally, I think they need an intervention, but I'm not the type to do something like that. Live and let live. That's a courtesy they extend to me as well, so we're good."

"I wouldn't know what that was like."

"What do you mean?" she asked.

"If my brothers and sisters weren't in my business on a constant basis, I would think the pod people had taken them over. They have their noses in every aspect of my life."

"Including your career?"

"Well, not what I do when I'm out in the field, but my

sisters really want me to quit special forces. They want me to settle down and join the police force or fire department like my brothers. I'll quote, '*Leo, if you have to risk your life, do it local so you can settle down with a nice girl and have bebés.*'"

Daisy snorted. "At least I never heard that from my siblings, or my mom or stepdad. I don't know what I would do if they told me how to run my life. I think I would fall over in disbelief. So tell me, have you got enough background on me?"

"Even your mom?"

"Especially my mom. Her parents were a big influence on marrying the good doctor so young. They thought it was a prestigious match." Daisy paused.

"What?"

She gave a half-laugh. "I was wrong. If anybody has an opinion about my life it's my grandparents. They're not impressed with what I've accomplished. They think I should settle down local and have some bebés."

Leo gave a full laugh. "I told you. There's always someone in the family with that opinion. Are you done massacring that eggplant? Can we order dessert now? And I'm not talking this damned tea."

Daisy's smile was a beautiful thing to behold.

"I'll take that as a yes."

"They use less sugar in their desserts. At least if they are truly like the ones that I've had baked for me by the Afghan women."

Leo made a gesture for the waiter, then requested the dessert menu. After he left, Leo asked Daisy to recommend something. She explained the different desserts, and he chose the sheer yakh which was basically the Afghan version of ice cream flavored with cardamom and wild orchid.

"I can't wait to tell my sisters I ate orchid ice cream. What are you having?"

"Gosh-e fil. It's a pastry that's lightly fried then topped with powdered sugar and other heavenly goodness."

When the waiter came back, they gave their orders. That was when Leo's phone rang. It was Kane. "I've got to step out and take this."

Daisy nodded. He was impressed she didn't ask a lot of questions.

As soon as he was out of the restaurant he answered. "Wait a minute."

"Okay."

The lobby was crowded, how in the hell had that happened? He went out to the front of the hotel, the heat blasting him like a furnace.

"Whatcha got?" he asked Kane.

"It's definitely the Haqqani Network, not Al Qaida. They've got the reporter and the doc. They're making noise about the doctor, they're pissed. He's been flying in the face of all sorts of Muslim laws. He's been treating women without their husbands present—"

"You've got to be shitting me."

"It gets worse."

"How can it get worse than that?"

"When confronted, he told Imans that they were trying to kill their wives and children. That they might as well be putting a gun to their heads, and that the prophet Muhammad would be ashamed of them."

"He did not bring up the prophet. Tell me he did not bring up Muhammad."

"Yep. He painted a neon yellow bullseye on his back.

Right now we have Marine translators on the ground, and they're trying to get intel from the Afghans or Taliban. Whoever they can, but they haven't hit pay dirt yet. Their feeling on this is that Dr. Squires is going to be made some kind of example."

"Beheading?"

"That's their take. Again, they don't have any intel yet. But yeah, most likely. The only thing stopping them is that our intel has the leader, Siraj Haqqani in Pakistan right now. They wouldn't want to do this without him to witness."

"But he's associated with the Taliban, and they want the Taliban to appear clean these days. I don't get it." Leo was confused.

"They wouldn't put Siraj on tape. He'd just be there for the joy of watching. Asshole."

"Oh, got it. What's keeping him in Pakistan?"

"Now *that* we do have good intel on. There have been some back-and-forths going on with the locals and the Haqqani. He's leading it. As soon as it dies down, you can bet he's hot-footing it to Afghanistan."

"So we've got to find Squires before the execution."

Great.

"Well, find him and rescue him." Kane clarified.

Double great.

"You left the embassy an hour ago. Did you get much from the daughter?"

"She basically confirms everything that you just told me. Her father is an arrogant prick who will sidestep all cultural norms to do what his pride demands. Arrogant motherfucker. It's going to end up getting him killed, and probably that reporter too."

"Get your ass to Bagram. We need to get a plan together."

"I'm still debriefing Ms. Squires."

"Do you think you're going to find anything else that will help us?"

Leo thought about it. "I might." Leo rubbed the back of his neck. "Give me twenty. If I don't get any more answers, then I'm on my way."

"Fifteen," Kane gave him.

"Fifteen," Leo agreed.

4

DAISY WATCHED LEO SIT DOWN AND LOOK FORLORNLY AT the empty dish of ice cream in front of her.

"It was melting. Don't worry, I ordered another dish for you."

"Did you eat that other thing too? The Oh-My-Gosh?" he asked.

She laughed. "I had them put the Gosh-e fil in a to-go box to take to my room for later." The waiter placed another dish of ice cream in front of Leo.

When the waiter left, he smiled at Daisy. "Thank you. I would hate to miss out on orchid ice cream." She watched his face as he took the first bite. He grinned.

"This is great. It isn't something I'm going to order at Baskin-Robbins, because nothing beats Rocky Road, but this is pretty damn good for flowery ice cream."

"You make me laugh a lot. Which is pretty amazing considering the circumstances."

Leo gave her a quick glance before concentrating on his dessert. Daisy took another sip of her mineral water and waited for Leo to finish his ice cream. She had a gut feeling that whatever his call had been about, she wasn't going to like it.

"What?"

"Just wondering who that was and what you talked about."

Leo scooped up the last spoonful and savored it. "Thanks for talking me into this." He sat back in his seat. "Yeah, we have some suppositions about your father, but nothing that's been confirmed so I can't share it."

She took a deep breath, trying to brace herself. "Is it because it's unconfirmed, or is it because it's bad?"

"Both. I'm going to leave in ten minutes, but I need to ask you a few more questions."

"Can I ask you one more?"

Leo nodded.

"Do you think there is even a little shot at rescuing my father?"

"There's always a chance. I wouldn't still be here asking questions if I didn't think we had a chance."

She leaned forward and rested her elbows on the pristine white tablecloth. "Okay, ask whatever you want, I'll answer anything. I've promised my siblings to do whatever I can to bring him home."

"Has your father ever consorted with terrorists to get sick people the care they needed?"

Daisy bit her lip. That was a tough one. How often had money that her charity had given women ended up in the hands of their husbands who were terrorists? How many times had a bride price been paid so that a young girl could be rescued from marrying some man at the age of twelve? If W.A.N.T. was doing that sort of thing, could her father be walking the same kind of thin edge to get kids the care they needed?

"You're thinking awfully hard over there," Leo said softly. He'd pushed his dish away and was watching her carefully.

"Is it always black and white in your world? It sure as hell isn't in mine. Trying to get the women the help they need in third-world countries has had some of my people making bad decisions instead of terrible decisions. But in the end, it has kept women and children alive, so ultimately my folks can look themselves in the mirror the next day. Do you know what I mean?"

Leo nodded solemnly.

It made her feel better.

"I don't know what my father has done. But I wouldn't be surprised if he has worked with terrorist organizations in the past."

"Do you think he might have this time?"

"I really don't know. I'd have to talk to Dr. Williams over in Pakistan to find out. However, from what I've heard it doesn't seem likely. This time he seems to have been intent on pissing off all and sundry just to get everyone inoculated. Why, what have you heard?"

"I really can't tell you, Daisy. Like I said, at this point, it's all hearsay."

She looked him dead in the eye. "So it's really bad shit."

He gave a short nod.

"Fuck." She knew what that meant. There wasn't going to be a ransom. Diplomatic channels wouldn't work. He'd done something that made the terrorists want to kill him.

She thought about her brother Jim. He was going to be devastated. Karen and Brian would mourn the loss of their dad, but Jim? Jim would spiral for sure. He'd gone into medicine, following in Ethan Squires' footsteps.

Granted, he didn't tour the world; instead, he worked in the lab, developing cures. But in his mind, he and his dad were working in tandem.

"Daisy?"

She shook her head, trying to get back to Leo and the conversation at hand. "I'm sorry, what did you say?"

"I said I had to go, but I'll be in touch."

"Okay," she breathed out slowly. She was still trying to take in all that Leo hadn't said, but really *had* said.

"Don't give up hope," he gave her a tight smile.

"Hope is practically my middle name," she quipped. "But I'm also a hardcore realist. I know what's going on. I'm going to the embassy again tomorrow. They need to lean on the Afghan government, who then needs to lean on the Taliban."

"Daisy—" Leo started.

She held up her hand. "I know that it is a Hail Mary play, but I've got to take it. You do what you do, and I'll play the only hand I'm left with. All right?"

He nodded.

"Don't you have to leave?"

He got up from the table and threw down enough Afghani bills to cover the meal and the tip. She scooped it up and tried to hand it back to him. "I'm buying," she protested.

"Not on my watch, you're not." He gave her the kind of smile that sparked every feminine cell in her body to attention.

She could imagine the pittance the Navy paid him. She tried again. "I insist." She tried to thrust the money at him again. He side-stepped her.

"You can pay next time," he winked at her as he took a step away from the table.

"In that case, there better damn well be a next time, Handsome."

He hesitated, then came back. "I promise, Daisy. There will be a next time."

"Don't think I won't hunt you down. That's another one of my superpowers, kind of like rattling cages. So you better keep your word."

His grin started out slow, but when it hit full blast, it was powerful. So powerful, she almost felt a force field hit her.

Whoa!

"I keep my promises, Daisy. I'll see you later."

She watched as he sauntered out of the restaurant. Her hand hurt. That was when she realized she still had the Afghani bills clutched in her fist. She dropped the money down onto the table, then called the waiter over for the bill.

By the time he'd gotten to Bagram Air Base, Leo had thought through his conversation with Daisy multiple times. According to Kane's file, Ethan Squires was quite the humanitarian, but clearly, he was a loser in the father stakes. Hell, the word loser didn't even begin to cut it. Looking at Daisy today, he'd easily imagined her as a toddler trying to 'fix' her mother and find help for her.

Then when she'd said that the hospital had 'eaten' her mother and she was sure her mother was dead, his heart damn near exploded with rage and pain. How could a father not offer comfort to his child? It was amazing that Daisy was here in Afghanistan trying to do anything to help the man. Her love for her siblings must be extraordinary.

As for what he'd done in Pakistan, that was information Kane had already gleaned, so nothing new there.

There was one thing that was gnawing at him. He did not think that Daisy would just sit on her thumbs in wait mode while his team gathered intel and formulated a plan. Plus there was the fact that even once they had a plan it wasn't like Leo would be able to tell her that the mission was a go. So, they had a live stick of dynamite back in Kabul who was going to do God knew what.

As he went through the myriad levels of security to get into the base, he coordinated with Kane to find out where his team had set up camp.

"Max has coordinated a closet for us to meet in. You'll like it. Hot, humid, and it smells."

Leo laughed.

He found the meeting room that was the size of a motel room. One of those motel rooms that you found on the side of the road at three a.m. when you couldn't keep your eyes open anymore. And it smelled even worse than one of those seedy pay-by-the-hour motel rooms. It could've just been him, though, after almost two hours in the heat on his motorcycle.

"How were the suits?" Max, his lieutenant, asked. "Anybody worth a damn?"

"Tom Ludlum was there. He has a little runt who's an absolute asshole working there at the embassy. I figure Tom's going to put him on the first plane home."

"Did you get a chance to coordinate with him?" Max queried.

"No. What's more, I'm not sure he has much to add to

the story. There were six men, which included the ambassador, all coming at our hostage's daughter. They were demanding to know if she had any idea if her father associated with terrorists. They were asking shallow questions, not getting to any real depth. It was a clusterfuck."

"What did she say?" Max wanted to know.

"She said exactly what his associate in Pakistan had told everybody, that he had been flaunting the rules, and if anything had been pissing off the locals—and as such, probably pissing off the terrorist cells."

"Why would they want to know if he was working with terrorists if he was kidnapped by terrorists? That doesn't make sense," Nic, the youngest of their team asked.

"Good question. Because they're idiots. But that wasn't what they were really after. They wanted her to stop all of the ruckus her family was causing in the States to get her father freed. It wasn't looking good for the government or for the officials in Afghanistan. She refused. Boy, did she refuse."

"What do you mean?" Raiden, their team medic asked in his normal thoughtful way. He had a gleam in his eye. Leo could tell he wanted in on the joke.

"They had no idea who Daisy was. None. Nada. They thought she was just the youngest child of the Squires clan, coming to ask the ambassador for help. She put up with their bullshit for only so long, then she stood up and slapped the desk and started growling at them."

Raiden's lip twitched. "Growling?"

"Honest-to-God growling. She stared them down, told them who she was, what she accomplished, and told them to basically get their shit together. It was a beautiful sight to behold."

Kane McNamara was the first man who started laughing, Cullen Lyons wasn't far behind. Of course, Kane started laughing first; his woman was quite the ballbuster. After they started laughing the whole team joined in. Even Max Hogan, their leader chuckled, which was rare for him; he was a pretty serious guy.

"But you ended up getting a sit-down with her, right?" Kane asked.

"Absolutely."

"How?" Cullen asked. "If she was such a ballbuster, why would she be willing to sit down and talk to you?"

"All I know is she left all those guys eating her dust, but as she was leaving the conference room, she winked at me."

Every man in the tiny room groaned. "Heartthrob does it again," Asher Thorne said with disgust.

"And don't you forget it. I know you all think it's the Italian Stallion with his curly hair and soulful eyes, but it's me. They love us Latin Lover types." Leo buffed his nails against his dusty T-shirt.

Again the men groaned, all except Ezio. "What, Ezio, you're not going to disagree?" Leo looked over at his Italian teammate. "You don't want to fight for your Italian Lothario status?"

"Hell no. I have Samantha, I already know I've won," Ezio smirked.

"Okay, boys, can it. I want to hear the real stuff. What did you find out when you got Daisy alone?" Max asked.

"She told me that if her old man has been in countries where it's been necessary to deal with the local terrorist organizations to get the people the care they needed, he wouldn't have batted an eye. The problem here is that a lot of the clerics aren't real down with his approach, which riles up the terrorists, so it makes him a target. She knows this. She's not wearing rose-colored glasses where her father is concerned."

"So he's all about the medicine. How do you think he's interacting with his captors? Did you get a read on that from her?" Max nodded.

"He'd be a stubborn asshole. There'd be no give," Leo answered.

"Great, just great. So that means the Haqqani Network will be chomping at the bit to kill him as soon as Siraj gets back from Pakistan," Kane said disgustedly. "The man doesn't have the sense God gave a gnat."

"That about sums it up," Leo agreed. "I worry what Daisy's next move is going to be."

Max's head shot up and his eyes pinned him. "What do you mean by that? She did her thing. She went to the embassy and demanded they act. What other play does she have?"

"I don't know. She's smart and determined. She couldn't have built up her charity the way she has without being willing to go over, under, and around any and all obstacles to get what she wants. She's not going to let the ambassador stop her from trying to get to her father."

"But she knows there is a rescue being planned, doesn't she?" young Nic asked. "I mean, it's kind of obvious that you're special forces."

"It better not have been," Max growled.

"Nic's right, it was to her. I told you, she's smart. She put it together by the time she was done shaking my hand. I didn't confirm nor deny any of her questions. She was adamant about knowing what our timeline was. That's what worries me. She's going to do something."

"Fuck," Max said as he ran his hand through his dark

hair. "We don't need this. Kane, call Tom and have someone put a tail on her, in case they haven't already. I want her watched in case she does something stupid. Okay, onto our next order of business." Max motioned for Kane to open up his field-grade laptop. That thing could withstand bullets and some minor explosions. And one time it had withstood Kane throwing it thirty yards in frustration.

"Hold on." Leo looked over at Raiden and grinned. They watched as Kane went into his duffel and pulled out a bulky sack. He loosened the draw string and took out a bunch of bubble wrap, which he carefully unwrapped until he got to his mini-projector. He might be brutal with his laptop, but his projector was dealt with like fine bone china.

He plugged it into his laptop, and images appeared on the far wall.

"Lights, Nic," Kane said.

Nic gave out a long-suffering sigh. Again Raiden and Leo grinned at one another. Even though Nic was closest to the light switch, in his opinion he was told to turn out the lights because he was the youngest. Max was going to have to pound some sense into the kid pretty soon and get rid of that chip on his shoulder.

"Aw fuck, caves." Cullen groaned.

"Oh for God's sake, Lyons, what else did you expect?" Asher demanded to know. "We're in Afghanistan. Of course, the terrorists would be hiding out in caves."

"They have bugs," he whined.

Everybody in the tiny room laughed, which is what Cullen had intended. Leo saw Max rubbing the back of his neck.

Shit, this was worse than he thought. Usually, Max didn't give away the game like this.

"Cut the crap, guys," Leo commanded. "What are we up against?" he asked Kane.

"Right now we know he's in the Pushtun Region of Afghanistan, we can extrapolate that their bases are in caves, which means the Hindu Kush mountain range," Kane explained. He used his laser pointer to show the most likely area.

"It's not going to be easy for Siraj Haqqani to get from Pakistan over to some cave in the Afghan side of the Hindu Kush mountains," Leo noted.

"There's always helicopters," Nic said. "But how often do they use them?"

"Not often, Nic," Kane answered. "But we can't rule it out."

"Nope, don't think so," Max said decisively. "Haqqani's going to know we're going to be carefully monitoring airspace because of the good doctor's kidnapping. He won't want to risk it."

"That's good news," Leo said. "Gives us three or four days to find and rescue Dr. Squires."

"Bad weather," Kane said. "So closer to four or five days. It gives us more time."

"Leo," Max pointed at him. "Go call Tom Ludlum, make sure that the daughter is being watched immediately. We don't need any problems on this side, we'll have enough to deal with on the mission."

Leo nodded and stepped out of the cramped office. He didn't have Tom Ludlum's number, but he wasn't worried. He pulled out his cell phone and waited. It took less than a minute and a text message from Kane came through with the man's number. Yep, their computer/communications guy sure could multitask.

He placed the call and got Tom's voicemail.

"Tom, this is Leo Perez, I'm with the Night Storm team, under Max Hogan. We've met before in Virginia and I was in the ambassador's office today during the poorly handled interview of Daisy Squires. I went to lunch with her this afternoon, I'm worried she's going to try to get involved. We don't need that. Can you make sure you have someone sit on her, to make sure she doesn't get into any trouble? Call me if you need details."

He hung up and went back into the conference room.

"—been reports of activity here." Kane was using his pointer at a specific spot on a close-up shot on the mountain range. He flipped to another slide which showed some drone footage. "This is what the camp looked like two weeks ago. Three men and two dogs. Now, look at it two days ago."

Leo did. There were two covered trucks and a jeep with netting over it, but it was easy to surmise that it had an anti-aircraft gun on the top of it. Leo also counted ten men, four dogs, and God knew how many were in the cave. They were taking their security seriously. Yep, something big was going on.

"We're going to set down here," Kane pointed to a spot a lot closer than any of the terrorists would ever expect.

Gotta love a Blackhawk helicopter.

"We don't have any diversion or specific timetable, so we're going to go in as soon as we can," Max explained.

"We're not going to make a play for Siraj?" Cullen asked. "Why not?"

"There's a reliable source close to him that says he'll be coming with an entourage of at least twenty. Yeah, it would be nice to take him out, but our number one mission is to get the doctor, and hopefully the reporter."

"Does the reliable source say if the reporter is with the doctor?" Leo asked.

Max shook his head. "All we got is the fact that Siraj is coming with a group of people. The higher-ups are not giving me anything as to who the source is, which is fine by me. So it could be coming from someone unrelated to the Haqqani Network in Pakistan, who just observed Siraj moving out, or it could be someone embedded in Siraj's organization. Either way, the brass is sure of the info."

Everybody nodded.

"Tonight?" Asher asked.

"Nope," Kane said. "The Blackhawks aren't available tonight, it's going to be tomorrow night. Raiden's sorted out where we're eating and sleeping, so get with him."

5

"I'VE BEEN WAITING FOR YOUR CALL FOR HOURS," DAISY complained into the phone.

"Calm down, Sweetheart. It took me a little while to get you the information you asked for. Are you okay? What's wrong?"

Daisy felt herself relax at the sound of her stepdad's voice. "Nothing's wrong, Dad, just a little tired."

"How about trying to pull the other leg, and tell me everything. I can't be of help if I don't know what's really going on."

Daisy sighed. The man was right. "I don't know where to start."

"You told me about the meeting with the ambassador and his men on the drive back to the hotel. You didn't sound so upset then, you sounded riled. Now you're sounding desperate. What has changed?"

"Remember the military man I told you about in the room?" Daisy asked. "He followed me to the hotel. He's special forces. I'll give you his info and I'd like you to get his details. In the meantime, he gave me enough broad strokes to let me know it's pretty grim for Ethan. I'd say they're setting him up for an execution."

"You can't know that for sure, Daisy."

"This guy is special forces. My gut is telling me that he and his team have been sent here to rescue him. You and the rest of the family are doing the right thing in the States by causing such a big stir, there is no way they would have sent in a team unless you were. They don't like to have their record blemished. Plus it's an election year. Can't have problems during an election year."

Daisy knew she was sounding bitter, but she couldn't help it.

"Provide me with the information on this man, and I'll tell you the source I have in Afghanistan for you. I believe he will be able to tell you what you need to know. Rayi is one of the few journalists who is still brave enough to send out reporting from inside Afghanistan. He would be killed if he were caught. He has agreed to meet you at a set time and place tonight. You only have one chance to meet him. He is very good and will know if you are followed, and if you are, he will leave the rendezvous."

"I am being followed, but it was amateur hour. It won't be a problem to get rid of them."

"Are you sure? They might have changed things up a bit after you've met with your special operations man."

Daisy thought about that. She pushed at the to-go container on her nightstand. "Okay, I'll do a trial run with my driver and see if anything's changed. Where and when am I supposed to meet this reporter?"

"You'll share a private car to the airport. You'll both be picked up from the Intercontinental Hotel at seven p.m. tonight and driven to the airport. That will give you plenty of time to talk. Rayi will have luggage for you at the hotel so that you can put it into the car."

"Got it."

"Now, tell me what has you so riled up. Obviously, it is the conversation you had with the soldier."

"SEAL. I'd bet my last dollar that he's a SEAL. Do you have something to write down his information?"

"Always," Alistair replied.

"Leo Perez, Chief Petty Officer. He's part of a team that's here." She paused and sucked in a deep breath. "Dad, I have the feeling that Ethan is going to be executed."

"Dammit. So he's been angering some locals," Alistair bit out.

"Yes. But don't tell the family. It will just upset them."

"I wouldn't, Honey. There isn't any point. I hate you having to know."

"I'm fine." And she was. She could handle it. That's what she did, put her feelings away and handled things.

"I'll have the information on your man very quickly, Daisy. I love you."

"I love you too, Dad."

She hung up.

It was four-seventeen. She called Malek. His wife had briefly worked for W.A.N.T.; that was the only reason Daisy had chosen him as her driver. She prayed that he was trustworthy.

"Malek," Daisy started the call with a smile in her voice.

"Yes, ma'am," he replied in Dari.

"I need your help. I think we're going to need another driver as well."

"I'm listening."

"I need to get rid of the people who are following me."

"That should be simple. They were already having trouble keeping up in our traffic."

"I think they might have someone better trying to follow us tonight. I have a plan I want to discuss with you."

"Yes, ma'am." This time she heard the excitement in his voice. All over the world, every man wanted to be James Bond.

ALISTAIR HAD BEEN RIGHT. Two cars were following them, and between them, Malek wasn't able to lose them, no matter how fast he drove, or how he wove in and out of traffic.

I'm not going to die. It will be all right.

She held on tightly to the St. Christopher medal that a nun had given her a couple of years ago. He was the patron saint of travelers and was supposed to keep you safe. At this point, she'd take any and all help she could get.

Daisy looked at her watch. It was five-ten. "Malek, it's time to go to plan B."

"Yes, ma'am."

Ten more minutes of Formula One driving and Malek screeched to a stop in front of the Golbahar Center Bank Mall.

"Will your nephew be ready for me?"

"Yes, he will."

"I'll look different," she warned again.

"It's okay, as long as you hold up your purse, he will come and get you."

She looked down at her bright red purse. Yep, it stood out. She was going to have to do something about that.

"They're here, ma'am."

Dammit!

Daisy bolted out of Malek's old car and strutted into the mall entrance. At this point, she wanted to be followed. She was immediately hit with the smell of perfume. She turned and saw the perfume store to the right. Next came a bigger shoe store. Neither of those would do. She needed a huge department store.

She meandered slowly down the walkway until she turned a corner and used the glass window of a rug shop to get a look at the man who was following her. Light blue windbreaker, chino pants, blond hair, and glasses. Nobody she recognized from the embassy.

She kept walking until she got to a rather large women's clothing store. It had both traditional Afghan clothes and Western clothing. Now it was time to see if she had any acting ability.

She slowly walked to the back of the store, stopping occasionally to look at different items on tables, but continuing to take note that the man in the windbreaker was just keeping watch outside the storefront.

"May I help you?" a motherly-looking woman dressed in Afghan garb asked in English.

Daisy worked up a helpless expression. She grabbed the woman's hand in both of hers. "I hope you can help me," she said in Dari.

The woman reassessed her. "What's wrong, my dear?"

"If you go to the front of the store, you'll see a man who has been following me all day. He knows my boyfriend is out of town on business, and he's," Daisy swallowed. Then she started again. "He's going to follow me to my home. I *need* to go to my friend's house without him seeing where I'm going."

The woman sighed. "And you can't go to the police," she shook her head sadly.

It was true. Both women knew that it was very likely the police would take the man's side.

"What can I do to help?" The woman asked.

"If I can change from Western clothes?" Daisy asked hopefully. "Perhaps one of your beautiful *parahaans* and *tombaan* sets, and left the store in disguise...?" She let her voice trail off as she looked around the store she saw the exquisitely handmade trousers and overdresses in subdued and bright colors, all with coordinating scarfs. If she wore the scarf low enough, she should be able to disguise herself.

The woman gave Daisy a thorough once-over. "It might work. We would have to get you the right shoes as well, and you could put your purse into one of the shopping bags." Now the sales clerk was getting into the project.

She hustled Daisy into a cramped fitting room, where she was met by many women laughing behind different curtains. This was obviously a fun outing for the ladies.

Before she had a chance to take off her blouse, the woman thrust three different garments into the fitting room. Daisy looked around to see where she could put them, finally seeing a hook. She snorted when she saw the price tags. The woman might be willing to help her, but it was definitely going to cost.

It was just as well. She needed to fit in at the Intercontinental Hotel, so high-end clothing was for the best. All of the clothes that the woman had picked out were rich and vibrant and beautifully made. Daisy chose the deep purple, and it fit like a dream.

Perfect. I'm outta here.

When the woman tried to thrust some more clothes into the dressing room, Daisy stepped out.

"I choose this," Daisy smiled.

"Excellent choice. I will get the shoes and *chaddar* to cover your hair. We can pin it here, so you will be unrecognizable."

Within five minutes, Daisy had just spent more on her credit card than a night at the Ritz Carlton in New York. Thank God Leo had paid for lunch.

"No, no, no. The *chaddar* is still not right," the woman said again. For the third time, she re-pinned Daisy's scarf, until none of her hair showed, and it flowed softly around her face.

The saleswoman looked at her critically. "You'll do."

She shoved Daisy's clothes and red purse into shopping bags. "Go out with a group of women, you'll be less conspicuous that way."

Damn, she was really getting into it. Maybe the Afghani woman wanted to be James Bond too.

Daisy stayed close to the entrance looking at a rack of clothes. When three women started to walk out, she walked close behind them, followed them to the left, and down the escalator. She looked up and saw the man in the windbreaker still standing in front of the women's clothing store.

I did it!

She glanced at her watch. It was six-twenty. She'd be cutting it close.

As soon as she was on the ground floor of the mall,

where all the food shopping was, she hurried to the south exit. How in the hell was Rayi going to recognize her when she got to the hotel?

One problem at a time, Daisy. First, just get your ass to the hotel on time.

When she got outside, she yanked her red purse out of the shopping bag and held it over her head.

Many drivers shouted at her to give her a ride.

"Miss Squires!"

She turned her head to the young man waving at her. He even looked like Malek. She hurried over to his car and got in.

"The Intercontinental Hotel."

"Yes, ma'am."

His tires actually screeched before she had a chance to put on her seatbelt. After she got it on, Daisy reached for her St. Christopher's medal around her neck and held on.

HERE SHE WAS AGAIN, in another hotel lobby about to meet another man who would hopefully have information about her father. She stood in front of the hotel gift shop, pretending to admire whatever it was they were selling. Her mind was so oblivious, she didn't even know what she was looking at.

"That's a nice watch, isn't it?" A man asked her. "Who would you buy it for?"

"My stepfather. I try to always get him something from every country I visit. But I would like something that is made here, instead of something that he could buy in the US."

"You are a good daughter. I believe our car is waiting."

Daisy turned to look at the man. They were of a similar height and she could look directly into his kind and intelligent eyes.

She smiled. "You're right, we don't want to be late for our plane."

Yay, I remembered my lines!

"No, we don't."

He indicated they were going back to the valet area, where the door was open, and he escorted her to the waiting limousine. She raised her eyebrow.

"This has a privacy screen," he quietly answered her unasked question.

She nodded.

The valet opened the door for her, and the driver opened the door for Rayi on the other side of the vehicle. After they were settled, the limousine began to move at a sedate pace. It was nice to not have to worry for her life for a change.

"How do you know my stepfather?" Daisy asked.

"I did a few humanitarian stories that interrelated with Tajikistan, and I needed corroboration. Your stepfather ended up pointing me in the right direction."

Daisy nodded, she could see Alistair doing that.

"So, do you have any information for me regarding Ethan Squires? Anything at all about what he might have been doing either here or in Pakistan?" It had finally occurred to her that the Haqqani Network spanned both nations and he could have just as easily enraged the Network on either side of the border.

He looked at her sadly.

"What? Tell me. What?"

"In Pakistan, one of the madrassas that he visited and inoculated children, was where Siraj Haqqani's nephew attended. It was lucky he wasn't killed while he was still over in that country."

"I know that. I'm also thinking it was either Dr. Williams or a member of his staff who tipped off Siraj that it was my father who did the inoculation. It's the only thing that made sense, since they wouldn't be sure which doctor did it."

Rayi nodded. "You're right, but before that happened, a member of the Taliban, who didn't want additional international trouble, told your father to immediately leave for the United States."

Daisy felt like her head was going to explode. Did her father have a death wish, why in the hell didn't he go home? What the hell had he been thinking? Fine, he did his normal shit, he ignored all common sense, risked his life, and put the life of Dr. Williams and the rest of his team in jeopardy.

Nothing changes.

"Why did the Haqqani Network wait until he was in Afghanistan to kidnap him?" Daisy asked.

"According to my sources, the one good thing Williams did was to give your father a running chance. He sent him over to Afghanistan before laying the blame at his feet."

"Yeah, like that was a nice thing since the Haqqanis have a hold over both countries."

Rayi nodded in agreement.

"Since Williams has a way to contact the Haqqani Network, I need to talk to him and see if I can get ahold of the same person. See if there is a way I can get a meet with Siraj."

"That's suicide."

"There has to be something he wants more than my father's death. We can get money."

"No. After what your father did, he will want to make an example of him. Your best bet is for someone to rescue him, or put pressure on the Haqqanis."

Daisy didn't want to give away that there was a potential for rescue, so she didn't say anything about that. "I don't suppose you know of any way to diffuse this situation with somebody else at the Haqqani Network, not Siraj?" she looked at him hopefully.

"The only possibility is the Taliban putting pressure on them. The Haqqani Network is still allied with the Taliban and the Taliban is trying to put itself forward as more of a government entity these days, not a terrorist organization. But it is doubtful that the Haqqanis will change their minds."

"How do I get a meeting with the Taliban?"

"I don't think you want to. Right now, it is a tenuous situation at best. All communication should go through proper channels, through your embassy to the Afghan government or directly with the Taliban."

"My embassy has been pretty clear that they won't do anything."

"The pressure that your family is putting on the American government back in the United States is helping. Soon the US government officials here in Afghanistan will have no choice but to have some under-the-table talks with the Taliban."

"But by that time, it will probably be too late, won't it?"

She waited for a response, and finally, Rayi nodded.

"So again, how do I get in touch with someone within the Taliban? Someone who won't kill me on sight?"

Rayi looked out the window. "We are almost at the

airport. I will call you tonight and see what I can do. In the meantime, go back to your hotel and wait for my call."

"Don't you need my number?"

"I have it."

6

LEO FOUND KANE AND MAX PORING OVER NEW SATELLITE images in the tiny conference room.

"They lost her," he said between gritted teeth.

"What?" Kane asked. "What are you talking about?"

"He's talking about Daisy. She managed to lose her tail. Goddammit, Leo, didn't you contact Tom? If he was in charge, there was no way she would have gotten away," Max said. He was clearly irritated.

But so was Leo. Actually, he was more than irritated, he was a little bit scared. What in the hell was that woman up to?

"Lieutenant, I know how to carry out an order," Leo said with his back straight and his shoulders thrown back.

"Can the 'lieutenant' bullshit, you know that pisses me off when we're not in front of the brass. I'm sorry I questioned you. But seriously, are you telling me that somehow Tom Ludlum and his team managed to lose one little girl?" Max was now irritated *and* incredulous.

Now Leo was feeling a tad bit of admiration. "Woman, sir, she is definitely a woman. You got to remember she's been all over this big wide world, kicking ass and taking names as she runs that charity of hers. Very few things stop her. I should have been more clear with him, that she'd be slippery."

Max rubbed the back of his neck. "You shouldn't have to have been. Tom wears big boy pants, he knows what's up, he should have figured that out for himself. How'd she lose him?"

"She went to a clothing store at a mall. They figure she went inside wearing Western clothes and came out wearing Afghani clothes, then took a different way out of the mall and a different driver. It was all planned out pretty slick."

"Dammit! What's she planning on doing?" Max always took his missions personally. That was just who he was. He was their leader and nothing escaped his notice. Of course, Leo was taking this pretty damned personal himself. When he thought of the petite, intelligent, beautiful woman he'd had lunch with earlier, his stomach lurched at what she could be doing out there.

"I don't know, Max, but you can be damn sure she's out there intelligence-gathering. She didn't have much for me today at lunch. She had a good idea of what kind of work I did. I'm telling you, nothing got by her."

"Obviously, if she was able to pick up on the fact that she had a tail. And, knowing Tom, he probably had two people on her," Kane said as he looked up from his monitor. "I've got her cell phone number, unless you already had it, Leo."

"No, I didn't get it from her," Leo admitted. "Maybe before she does something too crazy, I can get her to meet with us."

Max's head jerked up. "That is *not* a good idea."

"It might be, if she's planning something totally batshit crazy."

"Just get her on the phone," Max said. He was clearly resigned to the situation.

DAISY HAD CHANGED into jeans and a long-sleeved shirt and now sat in front of her laptop in her hotel room. She felt a little better after her shower. She hated waiting, even if there was something to occupy her time. God knows the e-mails had been stacking up like snow in Alaska. But almost all of the W.A.N.T. e-mails she forwarded to any one of her highly competent directors. There were a couple that she forwarded to the Chairman of the Board of Directors so they could discuss them in a few days. What she really needed to get to were the e-mails from her siblings and her mother. There was nothing from Alistair, but that was because he was going to be calling her.

Her finger hovered over her mother's name on the computer. Alice Barrett had a complicated relationship with her ex-husband. They had four children together. Most of the pent-up hostility that she might have laid claim to had been worked through over the last twenty years, but she was still an advocate on his behalf because three out of her four children cared for him so much.

Hell, there had been times she had tried to bridge the gap between Ethan and Daisy. She'd tried hard to make Daisy see the good in her father, but it had been like pushing a boulder uphill. When Daisy was fifteen, she and her mom had had a shouting match that could be heard all over the Tajikistan embassy. Alistair had to step in. After that, her mother had finally stopped trying to intervene. She'd left it for the lost cause it was.

Daisy opened her mother's e-mail first. She wasn't surprised by what her mom had to say. She told Daisy to not wear herself out trying to be all things to her brothers and sister. Her mother knew that Daisy would try every avenue to rescue their father, but that she mustn't beat herself up if she was unable to do so. She told Daisy to remember that her father had put himself in harm's way and that Daisy was not responsible for fixing this problem.

Daisy smiled wanly. It was a nice thought, but her mother didn't understand. She was the Executive Director of W.A.N.T., her unofficial job title was Maker of Miracles. She'd actually heard some of the women in her organization say that!

She and her team had helped get the money to ransom the girls from Boko Haram in Nigeria. Daisy along with others in her organization had gotten water wells drilled in the poorest villages in Zambia despite the government corruption. One arm of her organization that was just starting in Cambodia had just opened up a center for young girls and teens who had been sold by their families to brothels. These girls were severely physically and emotionally traumatized and needed a new start. It was Daisy's hope that with the new people she had brought on that they would eventually be able to stop some of the trafficking before the girls were sold into sex slavery. The idea of not being able to save her father was unacceptable.

Next, she opened the e-mail from her oldest brother, Jim.

Hey Sis,

I think we're really making progress over here. Brian met with a senator yesterday who seemed to think that the United States could get the Afghan government to do something. I don't know if that means negotiate with the terrorists or if they would do an attack. But Brian said it might be something.

But I'm not sitting on my hands. I don't trust our government to do anything, so I've been working with Davy. You know he has worldwide investments. He's working with an embassy that might do something for us if ours fails. You know what I'm talking about, sis.

Meanwhile, Karen is working with mom and Alistair to keep Dad's situation on the front page. She's managed to find one of his success cases to interview almost every day. Karen's making it look like Dad should be up for a Nobel Peace Prize.

I know Dad isn't always your favorite person, but what you're doing means the world to Brian, Karen, and me. If anyone can push the grunts on the ground there in Afghanistan to do something, it'll be you. We all love you, Daisy.

Love, Jim.

SHE OPENED up the attachments that he'd sent. She couldn't help but smile when she saw Freddie and Mikey grinning into the camera with their identical gap-toothed smiles. They'd even lost their front baby teeth on the same day. Talk about identical twins.

She adored her nephews. They had just turned four years old. It had only been three weeks since she'd last seen them, but it felt like forever. She needed to get back to the States.

Daisy opened up Brian and Karen's e-mails. They pretty much reiterated what Jim had told her, except for telling her about Jim's friend Davy. Now *that* situation scared the hell out of her. Davy was Deyvid Chubais, his father owned the largest bank in Russia, and Jim had performed CPR on Davy's mother-in-law at a restaurant years ago. They'd been friends ever since. If Jim was thinking of having Davy go to the Russian embassy for help, that was going to turn this into a circus.

She jumped when her phone rang. She looked at her watch, happy to see that Rayi was calling two hours earlier than she thought he would have. She looked at the number on the phone and frowned. It wasn't an Afghan number, it was a US number, and it wasn't any that she recognized. She thought about letting it go to voicemail, when she did the math and realized it was four a.m. on the East Coast in the States. *It must be important.*

She answered.

"Hello?"

"Hi, Daisy, this is Leo."

She licked her bottom lip.

"Well, this is a surprise. I'd ask how you got my number, but I'm pretty sure you wouldn't be able to answer, right?"

He chuckled. It hit every single one of her nerve endings and she shivered. Didn't she have other things that were more important to do than get turned on by some man she'd just met?

"I just wanted to touch base and see how life was treating you. Did you enjoy your shopping trip?"

This time she laughed. It was met by silence.

Good, maybe he's turned on too!

Stop it, stay on task.

"How come I'm not surprised you heard about my trip to the mall? Tell me, just how many cars were following me? More than the two that I spotted?"

"Nope, just the two."

How did he manage to sigh and laugh at the same time?

"I thought the CIA only wore windbreakers in the movies."

"I wouldn't know about that. I don't own a windbreaker," Leo said.

"Yeah, but you're special forces. A SEAL, right?"

"I thought we covered that at lunch," Leo said.

"We covered the fact that you're really good at side-stepping questions. Just like you did now. Since you're going to play that game again, I don't see any reason to stay on this call, do you?" She knew she was being a bitch, but she didn't have time for this shit. She needed to talk to Rayi and Alistair, then find out what the hell Jim was up to with Deyvid, because that could be scary as hell.

"Here I thought I was being cute."

"Nope. It was getting old. Are you going to start being straight with me?"

"Daisy, I'll be as straight as I can. Yeah, I'm a SEAL. Yeah, we're looking into how we can help your father, but I can't say much more than that."

"Help my father or rescue my father?"

"What's the difference?" Leo asked.

A brick that had been sitting on top of her chest lifted. The idea that Navy SEALs were planning a rescue had her breathing easier. It didn't mean she wasn't going to look at things from all angles though. Hope for the best and plan for the worst, that was her motto.

"Earlier you said it was bad. Are you going to act quickly?" she asked.

"That's another thing I can't answer. The when and how are need-to-know."

"So if you can't tell me anything, and I answered all of your questions at lunch, why the call now?" she asked him.

"Because you shook your tail this evening."

Daisy barked out a laugh. "I think that's a dance. *'Shake Your Tailfeather'*. Or did you mean something even more, shall we say, evocative?"

Leo snorted. "Don't get me started, Ms. Squires, I would like to be all sorts of evocative about your tail."

Daisy rolled her eyes; this was *so* inappropriate, but it felt good. "Look, Leo, let's get down to it, what do you want?"

I did not say 'get down to it.' How long has it been since I've been laid, anyway? Holy hell! Two years! No wonder everything coming out of my mouth sounds like a cheesy porn movie.

"Daisy?"

"Hmmm?"

"What did you do when you got away from the CIA?"

"It doesn't matter. I haven't found anything out that will help yet. Now that I have your number, I'll call you if things change."

I have to get off this call now. God knows what will come out of my mouth next!

"Daisy, we need you to stand down. We've got this under control. The last thing we need is you getting into trouble too."

"Leo, you know who I am. You know what I do. I'm careful. Thousands of women around the world depend on me. I'm talking about their very lives. I'm not going to screw this up. You can trust me."

"Then tell me what you were doing today."

"I told you, it came down to nothing."

"So far. There's a part two, right?"

Shit, how does he know that?

"There might be, but who in the hell knows. This is Afghanistan."

He laughed again. Daisy shivered...again.

"Can I get you to promise to fill me in if you hear anything that might make a difference? And I'm serious, Daisy, I need you to stay out of trouble. I also need any information that you might have that could help this situation."

"I don't plan to do anything that will put me in harm's way."

"I'm holding you to that."

7

LEO HAD TRIED TO GET AHOLD OF DAISY THAT MORNING, but no luck. The only good news was that Tom Ludlum had put a camera outside Daisy's hotel room and she hadn't left her room all night. She'd actually let in room service that morning, so Leo at least knew she was safe. *Still...*

"Perez, are you listening to me?" Kane wanted to know.

"Sure, you were going over the topography between where the Blackhawk is going to land tonight and where the cave is. It's hilly and rocky. I got it."

"Since you know everything, how about you telling us what you know, like what's so goddamn interesting on your phone?" Max asked sarcastically.

Leo thought he might lose it, which was just fucking stupid. He'd only met the woman yesterday, but he was acting like she mattered. Not that she shouldn't; everyone should matter, but she *mattered*.

"I'm seeing if Dr. Squires' daughter has tried for another escape, or if she has contacted me with any new information she might have found." At least he kept his voice level.

Nic laughed. "It was great that she gave the CIA the slip. I like her already."

"I'm right there with you, Kid. Any woman who can be that good, and that sneaky, is aces in my book. Hell, Kane, she reminds me of A.J. or maybe Eden," Cullen said as he turned his head to look at Asher.

"Not Carys?" Nic said.

"Carys would be in their face and demand they stop following her. It wouldn't occur to her to give them the slip. She would go all doctor on them." Cullen's voice held nothing but love and admiration for his fiancée.

Leo thought about it. Cullen was right. His woman was calm, cool, and collected, but when she was advocating for a patient she roared like a lion. Daisy would be like that too, he just knew it. But if subterfuge was more expedient, she would go that route, which is what she'd done yesterday.

"So, Tom has eyes on her? She's there at the hotel?" Max asked.

Leo nodded. "She said she would call me if she got any information that might be useful. She hasn't called, so I guess she didn't hear anything."

"Did you really think she would find out anything more than Kane would?" Max asked.

"I thought it was possible," Leo said. "She's a force to be reckoned with."

"If you feel like that, call her," Max said. "After the briefing."

Leo nodded.

Kane continued going over where they would be

landing and what they could expect according to the drone pictures.

"If things are set up as we've seen before, Dr. Squires should be held in the back of the cave. We have no idea how deep it goes. What would be best is if we could get them coming out of the cave instead of us going in," Kane explained.

"That's where I come in," Asher said as he stepped up and pointed at the map.

"Wait a minute," Raiden interjected. "Are we sure this cave doesn't link to any other cave or caves?"

Kane shook his head. "This is uncharted territory for us. There is no way to know. The drone has done an intense grid pattern for a kilometer around this area, and there is no other sign of life. No people or vehicles. So hopefully, this is the one and only hiding place."

Sounded like all possible recon had been done.

Max nodded to Asher so he would continue. "With Raiden's help, I'm going to set explosives under the jeep and two trucks. That will act as the diversion we need to get the terrorists to vacate the cave."

"But we don't think all of them will leave," Max said. "While Asher plays with C-4, Cullen, Nic, and I will be positioned on either side of the cave. During the chaos, we'll head in and look for Dr. Squires."

"What time is this going down?" Leo asked.

"We're expecting some bad weather from twenty-one hundred hours until zero one hundred hours, so we'll take off after that. Our ETA is zero two hundred. That would put us at the caves at zero three hundred.

Leo examined the topographical map. He glanced over at Ezio. As the team's snipers, it was their duty to find high ground so that they could cover everybody as they did their jobs.

Kane would monitor everyone's position on his laptop so that he could coordinate movements where needed. He'd be with either Leo or Ezio. If things fell to shit, Leo, Ezio, and Kane could go in.

"Are we going to get more shots of the target area?" Max asked Kane.

"They're planning another at eighteen hundred hours tonight, before the bad weather starts," Kane said.

"Who's coordinating this?" Max asked Kane.

"Captain Miller, USAF. This is what she does."

"Have you met with her?" Max asked.

"Yep. Did yesterday," Kane answered. "She knows her shit. The only downside is this is a new area to them, which is good and bad. Good, that they've now got something else nailed down. Bad in the sense that she doesn't know the area inside and out like she normally does. She's hating life. That's the reason for more drones and more photos."

Max turned to Leo. "Go make your call. Let me know if anything new pops up. I don't want any more surprises from the doctor's daughter."

Leo nodded, grabbed his briefing binder, and hauled ass out of the cramped conference room. It was only seven o'clock in the morning. The heat was already oppressive, but the outside fresh air still felt better than the stifling conditions of the indoors. He walked around the building and leaned his shoulder against a wall, then called Daisy.

"Hey, Handsome, aren't you calling pretty early? Weren't you worried you'd wake me up?"

"No, can't say I was."

There was a long pause.

"So, do you know exactly what I had for breakfast?" she asked with a hint of a laugh in her voice.

"Nope, just that you called for room service. Everybody on Team Good-Guy is happy to know that you're tucked safely in your room."

She chuckled. "Team Good-Guy, huh? I'm not sure I would want to be affiliated with those fucknuts that I had to deal with at the embassy yesterday if I were you."

"You have quite a way with words, Miss Squires," Leo smiled. He liked it. She cut through all the bullshit and didn't make him try to decipher what she was thinking and feeling, she just said what she was thinking.

"Just calling it the way I see it. So tell me, is the good-guy team part of the embassy clown-car?"

"Just one of the guys. He didn't do any talking. He was in charge of yesterday's tail. Now that he realizes just the quality of woman he's up against, he's upped his game."

"Tom Ludlum?"

Leo stared at his phone for a second.

"You know, you're kind of scary the way you get information."

"Leo, do you know what's really scary? The fact that Tom's supposed to be good at what he does and I still managed to lose his men. Anyway, they think they have me pinned in today, so they must be happy little campers," she exhaled slowly. "So tell me, Chief Petty Officer Perez, the man who was one of the top marksmen in SEAL Sniper School, what is on *your* agenda today."

"Whoever your information source is, they don't miss much, do they? Are you done showing off now?" he asked.

"Damn, you don't even sound a little bit pissed-off," she murmured. "I like that. Are you going to tell me what you're planning today?"

"Daisy, the only thing that's beginning to piss me off is that you haven't told me anything of significance. Before I side-step your questions, I've got more questions of my own." He heard her huff out a laugh. "Besides inoculating Siraj's nephew, did your dad, or any of his team, do anything else to piss off the Haqqani Network?"

"It's still the same crap we talked about at lunch yesterday."

"So, you came up with bupkis? I find that hard to believe."

"Why?"

"Because you would be out of your room doing something instead of in your room eating breakfast."

She let out a real laugh. "Okay, you're right. My contact is getting me a meeting with somebody he says he trusts. He's with the new arm of the Taliban who has been part of the ceasefire."

"Are you nuts?! Just what in the hell are you planning to talk about?" Leo felt his blood pressure triple.

"I'm going to see if we can offer Siraj money in exchange for my father. It was one of the things I promised my brothers I would try to do before I left the States."

"They're not going to go for it." Leo thought about how Squires had told the Imam that the prophet would be ashamed of them. There wasn't a chance in hell that anyone would go for ransom.

"I've got to try."

He had to stop this shit from going a step further.

"Daisy, it's more than just inoculating Siraj's nephew. He also invoked the prophet Muhammad's name when dealing with an Imam here in Afghanistan. He told the

Imam the prophet would be ashamed of him for not inoculating his family."

He heard her groan. "Please tell me you're making that up."

He didn't answer her.

"No, of course, you're not. That's just like Ethan Squires. He has to pour gasoline on every damned situation."

"So you see why meeting with this decent guy from the Taliban isn't going to do you any good, right?"

"I hate not having a back-up plan to my back-up plan. I know you Navy SEALs are supposed to be the shit, but Leo, something could go wrong. You might not find him to rescue him, have you thought of that?"

Again, he didn't say anything.

She sucked in her breath. "You mean you *have* found him?"

"Daisy, you can't meet with anybody from the Taliban. I'm going to tell Tom Ludlum to put you under house arrest."

"He can't do that," she protested.

"Yes, he can. He'll have two men put outside your door in minutes, and they won't let you leave your room. If you protest, they'll just take you to the embassy."

"Don't think I'm the only Squires out there trying to free my father. There are others trying just as hard and are just as desperate."

"What's that supposed to mean? Are one of your brothers or your sister coming to Afghanistan?"

"They don't have to be in Afghanistan to do something reckless."

Leo stood up straighter. "What are you talking about? Who's doing something reckless?"

"I can't tell you. It would betray a confidence."

"I call bullshit. You're too smart of a woman to just let that dribble out of your mouth unless you wanted to talk to me about it. So talk."

Leo swore he could hear her closing her eyes and resting her head back against a chair or the headboard or something. "You're right. I don't know how this is going to play out. But my brother has connections with somebody who can cut through a lot of red tape and get in with the Russian embassy here in Afghanistan."

Leo's stomach plummeted.

"Russia, the country that was paying the Taliban-linked militants to kill American troops, that Russia? Is your brother out of his fucking mind?"

"No, he's trying to figure out a way to start a dialogue with the Haqqani Network."

"Then he *is* out of his mind. They're killers, and your father managed to step right into the hornet's nest. Tell your brother to back off."

"I'm going to try."

"Do better than try, or I'm going to have to bring Tom Ludlum into all of this." Leo paused. "Dammit, that's what you wanted me to do, isn't it? That's why you're mentioning it, isn't it?" Maybe she wasn't as straightforward as he'd originally thought.

"Fuck, Leo, I don't know. I hardly got any sleep last night. I don't know if I'm coming or going, and my family is driving me insane. If you could just tell Tom that somebody is going to try to loop the Russian embassy into getting my father released through the embassy's Taliban contacts, without naming names, that would be wonderful. My brother's Russian connection isn't well-known, so I hope to God Jim's name won't be brought up in this."

"Fine, I'll talk to Tom. Maybe he can get our state department to tell the Russians it will be detrimental to their political standing if they get involved." He pinched the bridge of his nose. "But Daisy, just because you were able to lose your tail last night, doesn't mean you should underestimate these men. Once I tell Tom, he'll be searching for the connection. This could get your brother in trouble."

"For having a Russian friend?"

"If your friend is shady, and Jim has done anything shady with him, then things will get on the CIA's radar."

"Jim's clean. Trust me."

"Honey, I'm trying to. I really am. Go eat your breakfast, and I'll call Tom."

"Leo, you be careful out there. I know risking your life is what you do, but still, you just be careful, okay?"

"Always."

8

"HOW BAD IS THIS?" KANE LEANED OVER AND ASKED LEO.

Leo could hear the stress in Kane's voice. Some of it was because the last drone flyover that everybody was anticipating didn't come back with any good photos because of the sandstorm. But a lot of it had to do with the fucking weather.

Leo looked out the Blackhawk's gunner door's window. The dust wind that had subsided two hours ago before they had departed had suddenly come on strong again. If he had to guess it was damn near eighty miles an hour. The only good thing that Leo could see was that there weren't thick pillars of dust coming at them, but that's because of their altitude. God knew what it was like on the ground.

The pilot was going to have to determine what the situation on the ground was like before choosing to land. If it was impossible to see because of the sandstorm, then the smartest thing to do would be to abort the mission. Even with the synthetic vision system, there was too much of a chance that the wind could cause the helicopter to bounce around to hell and back, no matter how good the pilot was, and the surroundings had too many hills and big rocks to take the chance of landing without good sight.

"Kane, the only good thing we have going for us is that nobody will hear us coming."

"I love how this guy can see the bright side of every situation." Cullen grinned as he looped his arm around Leo's neck. "Too bad it's too dark for you to read a book tonight, huh?"

"Dumbass, when have you known me to read a book on the short hop to a mission? On the flight overseas, yes. On the helicopter ride to our target, no."

He'd brought *A Connecticut Yankee in King Arthur's Court* by Mark Twain this mission to read. He'd read that book as a kid, but as an adult, it was ten times better. He was midway through his second reading of it since they'd started the mission. If experience had taught him anything, he knew the pages of the paperback would be falling out by the time he was done, which is why he always started with a rubber band around the book when he brought it with him. Reading had been his passion since he started getting the highest kite on the wall for reading the most books in third grade.

The helicopter dipped hard down and to the right. Even in the dim light, he could see Asher swallowing hard. Put the man in the ocean, and he was golden, but give him a fuckload of turbulence and he had to force back the puke. Asher looked up and saw Leo grinning at him. He put up his middle finger. Leo laughed. Then the helicopter did another swoop. Leo looked at his watch, and did another look out the window. They should be at their landing site in fifteen more minutes.

He'd talked to their pilot Wilma before taking off.

She'd been flying Apaches and Blackhawks all over the Middle East for the last twelve years. They couldn't be in safer hands as far as Leo was concerned. As they got even closer, he was able to see the ground. Then he knew; Wilma would be touching down.

"Hold onto your butt, Asher," he said through their comm system.

He saw his friend gritting his teeth. It wasn't nice to laugh at his friend's suffering, but hell, everyone on the team was laughing. Asher would just have to suck it up. When it came down to it, everyone had their time at bat providing entertainment to the team. Tonight it was Asher Thorne. Bless his heart. The weird thing though—Asher was happy as a lark jumping out of a plane. He'd do that five times a day, just fine. *Go figure.*

"I'm setting us down, gentlemen," Wilma's voice came over the comm system.

"She sounds hot," Nic's voice was filled with enthusiasm.

"She is hot," Leo concurred. Any woman who could fly through this shit was hot in his book. Not as hot as Daisy, but hot, nonetheless.

Just as they were about to touch down, the helicopter did a hop to the left because of a strong gust of wind. Still, it didn't stop Wilma from nailing the landing.

Kane did one last quick check on everybody's commlink, then they put on their night vision goggles and headed out.

"I'm proud of you, Bubba," Leo heard Cullen telling Asher.

"Go fuck yourself."

"Seriously, you didn't puke all over Wilma's Blackhawk. You're such a big boy."

Everybody but Nic was able to keep from laughing out loud.

"Can it, Lyons," Kane whispered after they went over the first big rise. This was pretty much how all their missions started—Cullen being a smart-ass until Kane or Max shut him up and that's how they knew that they were on radio-silence.

They had five kilometers of hills and rocks to get over before he and Ezio would start looking for the best points for them to set up. They'd agreed ahead of time, it would be good to try to get no more than fifty meters apart and no less than twenty meters for the best sniper coverage.

Wouldn't you know, the sandstorm had pretty much died down as soon as they'd touched down. Now they were heading to the cave at a steady but quick pace. Asher and Max were taking the lead, scouting out for anyone who might be on watch.

After three kilometers Leo eased closer to Ezio and pointed to a high peak. There was another one a little lower that was forward and to the right. Ezio gave Leo a thumbs up. They started to move faster, wanting to determine if these spots had a view of the cave—according to Kane's coordinates, they should.

They caught up with Max and Asher and pointed to the peaks. Max nodded. Ezio headed toward the higher on the left. Leo started toward the one on the right, with every footstep he started to get in the zone. He mentally saw himself setting up his rifle, training his scope on his target, taking a breath, depressing the trigger.

By the time he got to the edge of the peak, he was ready. He took a look over. In the gloom, he couldn't make out much, even with his night-vision goggles. He got out his rifle scope. Then he saw the mouth of the cave and only one truck.

Fuck.

"Only one truck," he whispered into his mic.

He would bet his bottom dollar that the doctor had been moved, but they were going to have to try. Maybe they would get lucky and find a clue, or better yet, somebody they could get to talk.

"Stick to the plan," Max whispered.

Leo used his scope to search out Ezio. He was already planted with his rifle, ready to take on all-comers. Leo was late to the game. He got set up fast. Once he was, he could see Max and Archer creeping up like shadows to the perimeter of the cave area. Max made a hand motion and Cullen and Nic immediately came up from the shadows. Nic and Cullen went to the left side of the cave where the truck was, Max went to the right side.

Kane came up beside Leo, his computer at the ready as he looked over the ridge with his binoculars, then back down at his open computer.

Raiden was the last to the party. He got into the bed of the truck, ensuring it wasn't booby-trapped. "It's clean back here," he said. *Well, at least they hadn't departed and left us with some sort of parting gift.* Raiden joined Max.

Asher was already underneath the truck, planting bombs of his own. He scrambled out from beneath the truck then he ran to Cullen and Nic.

"Three, two, one," Asher breathed into the mic.

The explosion shot outwards, away from the cave, just as Asher planned. It was less than twenty seconds before the first man ran out from the cave. Max grabbed him and yanked him back, out of sight of the mouth of the cave. The man lifted his pistol, then Max shot him. Three more men exited the cave, all shooting. Leo aimed and shot one while two more went down by others.

As expected, nobody else came out. Instead, shots fired outward from inside the cave.

Max hit the ground and peeked around the edge, his gun ready. He wasn't going to take any indiscriminate shots, in case either the doctor or the reporter were inside. Leo moved, turned his rifle barrel, and saw that Cullen had done the same thing on the left side of the cave. He could see that Cullen was taking shots.

"They're down," Cullen said.

"Affirmative," Max said.

Nic and Raiden went in as Cullen and Max continued to cover them.

Leo hated this. He trusted his teammates—they were fucking indomitable—but still, he wanted to be the one taking the risks, not them. And if he couldn't be taking the risks, then he wanted them to be giving him a play-by-play of what was going on. Instead, it was dead quiet.

After what seemed like an eternity, there was a shot.

Then another.

Another.

He heard a man scream.

Two more shots.

"Down!" It was Nic's voice. He must have been shouting at Raiden.

Three more shots in rapid succession.

Another scream.

Absolute silence. It was deafening. It seemed to stretch on forever. Leo always wondered how in the hell Max stood this, not demanding that Nic and Raiden report into him.

"We're clear. No more tangos." Nic said.

Asher began checking the bodies outside the cave to ensure nobody was alive. Cullen went into the cave to ensure all of the 'dead' were dead.

"We've got signs of a prisoner having been held here, at some point," Raiden said.

Leo broke down his rifle, looked over, and saw that Ezio was doing the same thing.

"Kane, they left a camera tripod," Raiden said.

"Guys, we've got to go. Another weather system is coming in," Kane said. "We've got to move."

They made fast time getting back to the helicopter. As soon as Wilma saw them, she started up the bird. There was no laughter as they headed back to Bagram.

"Tripod?" Kane said to Raiden.

"Yep," came the subdued response.

"Chances there's a video out there somewhere. Don't know of what, if there wasn't a body," Kane said. It was clear he was confused.

"Kane," Leo started. "Do you think it was possible that they were doing an internal message between just the Haqqani Network?" Leo paused. "Or maybe something to Siraj?"

"I can't understand why a tripod. Why not just film it with their phone?" Nic said.

"Nope, they try to make these really pro. They're going to be pissed when they find out they left it behind. But in answer to your question Nic, they do use their phones, they just put it on the tripod," Kane explained.

By the time they got back to Bagram, they were whipped. After they cleaned up, Max had found them an even tinier closet to meet in since, even at six o'clock in the morning, the smelly larger conference room was taken.

"You did good out there." Max took a moment to look each and every member of his team in the eye. He didn't need to say or do more than that. Coming from Max Hogan...well, it was the highest praise you could ask for. Not even hearing something from an Admiral could make you feel better.

Max then turned to Leo. "I've been thinking about what you said, Leo, and I think you're on to something. We know that they're not going to kill Squires until Siraj is here in Afghanistan, so maybe they wanted to upload something on a website just for them, or send something to their leader."

Kane pulled his laptop out of his duffel. "I'm on it."

"All of you, including you, Kane, go find a bunk and get some shut-eye. Tomorrow's another day. We're going to find these sons-of-bitches."

Leo laughed when Max pulled the laptop out of Kane's hands. "No more toys for you."

"But, Dad," Kane whined. "Just a little longer."

"You can have it back in the morning."

9

DAISY WOKE UP TO THE SOUND OF HER LAPTOP SQUAWKING at her. It was a Skype call coming in. She looked at the phone on the nightstand and saw it was nine a.m. She bolted out of bed; how did she sleep so late?

She scooted over to her computer. It was Rayi.

She looked down at herself. She was wearing a Chicago Cubs T-shirt, no bra, and panties. She carefully positioned the laptop's camera so he would only see her face.

She answered the call.

"I have good news," he started.

"My father's been rescued?" Daisy was ready to jump out of her chair.

"No, but we know he's still alive. One of my colleagues monitors a chat room where the Haqqanis communicate."

"Why haven't we used that to talk to them?" Daisy wanted to know.

"It would blow the cover he has spent years cultivating. He cannot do it. But what he has done is discovered a video of your father from yesterday."

"He has? Can I see it?"

"Yes, I've downloaded it to the secure server you provided to me. I must warn you, Miss Squires, he does not look well, but he is alive. That is the important thing to remember."

"Trust me, I know that is the important thing. This is such good news! Are there any clues in the video as to where he's being held?"

"None that I or my colleague could see."

"Thank you, Rayi, I appreciate it."

"You're welcome."

He signed off and she immediately went to the secure server. It took her just a moment to find the video. She opened up the video file and pressed play.

To begin with, she couldn't see much; the focus was all blurred, and the camera was moving. Then it stopped moving and the camera came into clear focus. Someone shoved her father onto his knees in front of the camera.

"No," she gasped. His face was mottled with bruises. There was dried blood at his temple, his jaw was so swollen she wondered if he could talk.

She traced her fingers over the computer screen as if she could touch him. As if she could somehow help him.

"My name is Ethan Squires. I tried to help the people of—"

Daisy watched in horror as the butt of a rifle came into view and hit him in the head. He crashed to the ground, a gash opening on the side of his head, blood pouring out. A voice from off-screen screamed at him in Arabic, telling her father not to lie. That he was an infidel who had sinned against the prophet. Somebody rushed to lift her father up. He was wearing a face covering as well as his *keffiyeh*; there was no way to tell who he was. He tried to get her father to kneel up on his own, but it was a lost cause.

More screaming in Arabic ensued. Swearing he would kill her father if he tried to fake an injury, telling him to get up and tell their leader how he had betrayed Muslims everywhere. The man was holding on to her father's elbows. They were yanked up almost to his head. He was groaning in pain.

"Tell them," the man kept shouting from off-camera. "Tell them your sins."

"I did nothing wrong. I tried to help."

Daisy cried out when she saw the butt of the gun come flying on-screen again, but this time the man holding her father yanked him out of the way.

"No. You'll kill him," the man cried. "Our leader wants him alive for the beheading."

"He must repent," the man yelled from off-screen.

Daisy kept her eyes glued to her father and saw the moment he passed out. She gasped out a breath and that was the moment she realized she'd been holding it.

The screen went black. Her whitened fingers were touching it while harsh sounds were coming out of her mouth. She tasted salt. *What's happening to me? What's happening to me?*

"Oh, God."

She practically fell out of her chair as she rushed to the bathroom. She pushed up the toilet seat just in time to throw up. She heaved and heaved until there was nothing left in her stomach, but still, she heaved some more.

Daisy blindly reached for the toilet paper, wanting to wipe away the snot, tears, and saliva.

Suck it up, you've seen worse.

Her stomach heaved again.

She tried to think.

Why can't I think?

She hit the tiles on the floor with her fist, happy when she felt the pain.

Think!

She shuddered, and hated it. She tried to push herself up from the floor but found her legs too weak.

Pull yourself together, girl!

Daisy heard her phone ringing from the other room but she couldn't handle it. She just couldn't handle it. Let the world spin on its own without her for a while. It didn't matter.

I shouldn't care!

She hit the tile again with her fist.

That's why I came here instead of my siblings. I wasn't going to care; it was just another job.

She tasted salt again.

She closed her eyes. She could do better than this. She'd always done better than this. Emotions screwed up every assignment. She couldn't afford to feel them or they'd stop her in her tracks. Make her powerless. People suffered when she was powerless.

She closed her eyes and tried, desperately tried, to relax her shoulders. It wasn't working, but she took a deep breath in, tightened her shoulders, then let out a slow breath and relaxed her shoulders.

She felt them relax a tiny little bit.

She did it again.

Then she saw her father's bruised face and the gun hitting him. She winced.

She heard her phone ring again and forced herself up from the floor. Going to the bedroom, Daisy grabbed her phone and turned it off, not caring who was calling. She slammed her laptop off and unplugged it.

The world can wait. The world can just fucking wait.

———

Something was wrong, Leo could feel it in his bones.

Could just be the fact that they'd just seen the video of Ethan Squires, but unfortunately, that was almost to be expected. Every single one of the Night Storm team was just thankful that the man was alive. They still had time to rescue him. Now it was just a matter of finding out where he was.

But that still didn't explain why Leo was sure that something was wrong.

"Any word on our next target?" Leo turned from Kane to Max.

"We're supposed to hear something tomorrow morning," Max said. "The higher-ups are being cagey. They have a source they're really trying to protect."

"If this source is able to lead us to Squires, well then, they're worth protecting," Leo said.

"In the meantime, more drones are going up and looking for that jeep with the anti-aircraft gun. If they can spot that, it would give us a good indication that Squires is there."

"They can't have gotten too far," Asher said.

"We're not sure that others with trucks didn't come in and load them up. We can't just assume that that one truck and jeep were their only means of transportation," Max explained.

He's right, Leo thought.

"We're going to get some training in. Nothing like

some good one-hundred-and-twelve-degree heat to get a body moving," Max grinned.

"My money's on Kane falling behind first. He's the oldest, I think the heat will do him in," Raiden said with a grin.

"Nope, Max has me by a month, he's going down. What's more, he skips out on training back at Little Creek. He keeps saying he has paperwork to do. Nope, it'll be Max for sure." Kane closed down his laptop. He was definitely getting into the mood.

"Based on all this trash talk, and the fact that I'm the best and the youngest, all y'all are going down," Nic was practically blowing smiles out of his ass.

"A baby like you hasn't developed the endurance," Ezio razzed him.

Max looked over at Leo. "What's with you, Perez? I expected to hear from your corner of the world."

"I've got a bad feeling. I've tried to get a hold of Daisy four times today, but nothing."

Max gave him an intent look. "Do you think she's skipped out of the hotel again?"

"Nope. I checked with Tom, he said that not only do they have the camera on her hotel room, they have her door tripped, so if it opens they're alerted. It hasn't been opened."

"If she's as good as you say she is, maybe she disengaged it," Kane suggested.

"God, I hope not." Leo pressed his fingers against the bridge of his nose.

"Shit, you're going to be useless out there today and you'll lose, and you'll say it's because you were worried about the doctor's daughter, so we won't even be able to rub it in," Max sighed. "Get the hell over to Kabul and check on the woman."

Leo brightened. "Yes, sir." He didn't need to be told twice.

"Don't take the motorcycle, take something that won't kill you."

"What's the fun in that?"

"Leo." Max's tone brooked no argument.

DAISY PUSHED her head under the pillow. Anything to make her head stop hurting and the ringing stop.

It didn't stop.

God, she felt hungover. She clasped the pillow with both arms and surrounded her head with it so that her ears were covered. Finally, some relief—she couldn't hear the ringing. She didn't remember drinking, but her mouth felt like somebody had planted six acres of cotton in it, stinky cotton. It felt like her brain had grown three times its normal size and was trying to burst through her skull.

What in the hell had happened to me?

Now there was pounding, not ringing.

Her dad. Now she remembered. Ethan. The blood and bruises.

She squeezed her eyes shut tight and whimpered but it didn't shut out the pounding. She thought she heard someone calling her name.

What?

Daisy lifted the pillow off her head and that actually helped. Who knew a feather pillow could be so heavy?

"Daisy, are you all right?"

Pound.

Pound.

Pound.

"Open the door, Goddammit."

Thud.

Thud.

Thud.

It was Leo. And he sure was making his presence known. She staggered out of bed. She was halfway to the door when she realized what she was wearing.

Fuck it. Like Leo hadn't seen some woman in a man's T-shirt before.

She opened the door and he stared at her.

"Jesus, Daisy, what happened to you?"

"You get laid with that kind of sweet talk?" she muttered as he shoved his way into her room.

"What did you just say?" he asked as he shut the door and turned her around so he could get an even better look at her. If she'd been feeling better, she would have yanked herself out of his hold, but she wasn't, so she just stood there staring up at him.

"Honey, answer me, what happened? Has somebody hurt you? What happened?" His questions came at her like bullets. It was too much.

"Stop it! Just stop it! I can't think."

She whirled away from him and went to stare out the window, clasping her arms around herself, trying to keep herself together.

Then he was there, behind her. "Shhhh, I'm so sorry. I didn't mean to come on so strong." His breath tickled her hair. "I'm worried." He eased himself between her body and the window and crouched down so that they were at eye level. She looked into those deep brown eyes, so full of concern.

She shook her head, her hair flying everywhere. It stuck in her mouth. "There's nothing you can do for me. I'm behaving like an absolute idiot," she gulped. As soon as she took that deep breath, she shuddered, and her eyes began to well up.

"Ahhhh, Daisy." He stood up straight and pulled her into his arms. She stiffened, but Leo wasn't having any of that. One of his hands was rubbing her back and began to soothe her, while his other hand held her head in such a delicate grip as he guided her cheek against his chest.

Daisy knew she shouldn't be allowing this; she should handle this on her own like everything else. But God, it felt so good.

"Baby, you're trembling, can you talk to me?"

She shook her head.

"Okay. Okay. I've got you." He held her closer.

What was best? The warmth of his body that was helping to stop her chills? The feel of his strong arms enveloping her body, so that she felt nobody could get to her? Or was it that smell of sunshine and man that was uniquely Leo?

She snuggled closer and listened to his steady heartbeat, and decided that was the best thing, having another human being to share the storm.

How long did they stand like that in front of the window? Until it got hot.

Daisy felt the soft brush of Leo's lips against the top of her hair. In her adult life, she had never met a man who made her feel so cared for. How was that possible? She'd only known him for seventy-two hours.

She moved her hands to push away from him, but instead, her fingers dug into his white T-shirt.

What am I doing?

God, she didn't want to push him away, she wanted him even closer. She needed him closer.

She threw back her head so she could look up into his eyes.

"Are you ready to talk about it?" he asked soothingly.

"Kiss me."

His eyes widened just a bit. "Daisy—"

"I know what I want. I know what I need. I know *who* I need. I need *you*, Leo. Inside me. Now. But I'll settle for a kiss to start."

His hand stroked her hair back from her forehead. "I think you're emotional and you need to talk."

Emotional was something Daisy tried never to be. "We'll talk," she promised him. "After." Then she frowned. "Unless you don't want me."

"Fuck, Daisy, you're kidding, right? Of course I want you. I've practically had a hard-on for three days just thinking about you. But this doesn't feel right when you're upset."

"This is exactly what I need. It'll make things better for a while, and then we can talk, but I can't right now. I can't talk. Okay?" She heard the trembling in her voice, and she wished she could stop it, but she couldn't.

Really, was sex too much to ask for? He tipped up her chin and she looked into his assessing gaze. Fine, let him see for himself that she was serious. That this was exactly what needed to happen.

"You promised me a kiss. Let's see where it leads."

His thumb brushed against her bottom lip and that one touch zinged to every nerve throughout her body.

10

DAISY WAS SHATTERED AND LEO DIDN'T WANT TO TAKE
advantage. At the same time, he knew what it was like
when the only thing that would push the darkness away
was sex. But he didn't want to be some meaningless fuck
in Daisy's life.

Then you better make this a damn good kiss, Perez.

He looked into her glistening gray eyes. He bent at the
knees just a little because Daisy was so damned petite,
then he kissed the corner of her mouth. She moved her
face, trying to capture his mouth for something deeper.
He chuckled.

He brushed his lips against her jaw.

"No, I want a kiss."

"I am kissing you," he breathed against her ear.

"A real kiss."

According to his dick, this was a real kiss. He slid his
mouth down her cheek, inhaling the scent that was
uniquely Daisy. And salt.

Shit, she's been crying.

She reached up and grabbed his hair, angling his head

so that their lips met. She thrust her tongue into his mouth. He stepped sideways so that he could keep his footing. God, she was going to be the death of him.

Her taste exploded in his mouth, through his head, his body, and settled in his heart.

Daisy.

He caressed her dainty tongue with his, savoring the velvet texture and how every stroke took him higher and hotter than he'd ever been. Daisy stepped forward, her stomach pushed against his erection, and he knew damn well it wasn't an accident.

He felt her nails dig into the back of his neck; the little girl was seriously serious. Which was fine by him, but every so often he tasted tears. So, he was going to take control and do things his way.

He bent his knees even more and caught her up in his arms.

She wrenched her mouth away from his. "What?" she stuttered.

"We're doing this right." He looked over at the bed that looked like a tornado had hit it. Which was fine, they weren't going to be needing any covers. With her securely in his arms, which felt so right, Leo strode over to the bed and yanked back the duvet and top sheet and threw them to the floor, then gently lowered Daisy to the bed.

He turned away.

"Don't go," she pleaded.

"I'm not going anywhere, Sweetheart, I promise." He went to the window and shut the sheers so that they had privacy but still let in the light. He went over and cranked down the AC and checked for the third time that the door was locked. Daisy was lying up on her elbows, watching him. She had a vulnerable look on her face. It killed him.

"Okay, this stops here, Honey."

"What?"

He sat down on the side of the bed and cupped her cheek. "I know something bad happened, and you're looking for some way to put it behind you. I get that. Hell, I've been in your shoes, no judging here. But now it looks like you've changed your mind, and that's okay too."

She struggled to get into a sitting position and when she did her eyes were spitting fire. "Well, I'm sure glad there's no judgment on your side. This isn't just some mindless need to have sex with the first man who walked through the door, Leo Perez. I don't know what in the hell you've done in your past, but I've been a whole hell of a lot more discriminating and I've wanted you since I saw you in the embassy, but I've really liked you since we had lunch."

Leo couldn't help but smile.

"Damn right you should smile. Not many men make it into my bed. I might be using you for the moment, but I was planning on doing this before I got all upset and needy. But by all means, let's call this off..." her voice shook.

Ahh, God, he could see tears beginning to form in those storm-cloud-colored eyes of hers. He pulled her into his arms again.

"Daisy. My Daisy. You're damn right you were going to end up in bed with me. It was destined since the embassy conference room."

She didn't say anything as she burrowed in closer, her face tight against his neck.

This time he wasn't going to fuck it up. He was going to make love to this beautiful woman, then he was going to get her to open up to him. He cupped the back of her head and tipped her back for another one of those soul-defining kisses. But before he got too lost, he reached down with his other hand and started to untie his boot laces. He needed to climb into bed with her. Right. Now.

She pulled away. "What are you doing?" her eyes were dilated, and almost black.

"Taking off my boots."

She smiled brightly. "Good idea. Naked." As his fingers were working on his bootlaces, she began to work on the fastening on his pants, which was not helping a damn thing!

"Daisy, I need to get my boots off first before I can get my pants off," he complained.

"You're not fast enough," she purred.

He looked down at her flushed, smiling face and grimaced. Yep, she was going to be the death of him. "Why don't you stand over there by the desk and very slowly take off your sleep shirt? Very, very, very slowly," he suggested.

Her smile turned sexy. She slid off the bed, while he watched and fumbled with taking off first one boot and then the other. He tossed them across the room, then his socks. He stood and grabbed his wallet out of his pants and put it on the nightstand so he'd have the condom ready, then he stood stock still as Daisy started to sway side-to-side, as she began lifting the sports shirt up and up and up, over her tummy, so that her breasts began to show, then he saw the most beautiful pink nipples. He kept looking between her face and her breasts and her white panties, and back again. He was on overload.

Daisy knew it too. He could tell by the look on her face she was enjoying putting on a show for him.

"Take it off," he demanded in a husky voice.

"Make me."

Oh, he wasn't about to do that. It would ruin the fun.

He sat down on the bed and narrowed his eyes, watching her intently. She swayed even more.

"You're gorgeous. I can't wait to see all of you. Your skin is beautiful, it gleams in the sunlight. Your breasts are perfect, songs could be written about your breasts. But Honey, it's your sultry smile that does me in. Take off your shirt and come to me."

She slowly pulled it over her head, and her brown hair tumbled down around her shoulders. There was no hesitancy in her eyes. She was a woman who knew what she wanted and wasn't afraid to go after it. He was enthralled as she sauntered over to him.

"Stand up," she commanded.

Of course, he did. She looked up at him. "We're doing this, right?"

"Oh yeah," Leo agreed. He put his hands on her shoulders and stroked them down her arms until he tangled his fingers with hers. Such small hands that took care of so much. Her lips were shiny, plump, and pretty. Leo couldn't resist the invitation.

He bent his head and took all she offered. He licked at her lips, tasting her, savoring her. When she didn't immediately open, he gently nipped at her plush lower lip. She gasped and he took advantage, thrusting his tongue inside the warm cavern of her mouth. Kissing Daisy was like jumping out of a plane, only better. Over and over she rubbed her tongue against his, and his blood heated, his head spun. Leo released her hands and cupped her face, his thumbs caressing her cheeks.

He pulled away for just a moment. He had to tell her... "*Eres gloriosa.*"

"You're the glorious one," Daisy said, as she pulled at the hem of his T-shirt. "I want to see you, Leo. I need it."

He caught the note of desperation in her voice. Then he remembered how he'd found her. He pulled his shirt over his head. Once again she was working on the fastening of his pants. He heard her mew of frustration. As confident as she seemed, apparently she wasn't adept at undressing men. For some reason that made Leo smile.

"Honey, it'll be faster if I do this."

"Fine," she said, clearly irritated.

Leo pulled off his pants and briefs in one fell swoop. He bent and picked her up once again and placed her on the bed.

"I know you're strong and I'm small, you don't have to keep proving it."

"I'm not trying to prove anything. It's just expedient to put you just where I want you." He put one knee on the bed and stroked his fingers from her throat, between the valley of her breasts, down her stomach to the top of her panties.

"I think these can go, what do you think?"

"Definitely."

Slowly, he pulled the white cotton down her legs, exposing her pretty brown curls, with a hint of glistening pink.

As he pulled them all the way off, he couldn't help but notice her siren-red toenails, so at odds with her no-nonsense lack of make-up and unadorned fingernails. It was like she hid this little bit of femininity and he was lucky enough to see it.

He picked up one dainty foot and kissed her arch.

"No, kiss *me*," she protested.

"I am."

He spread her legs so that he could crawl up the bed and lay between them. He wrapped one arm around her head and stared at her delicate breasts, which were perfect for her petite body.

"You're staring."

"I'm just planning my attack, your body requires thought."

She smothered a laugh.

He cupped one breast as he licked around the swollen nipple of her other breast. Warm, plump, and a flavor that was all Daisy. He twirled and swirled his tongue around the turgid tip, while his hand lovingly caressed and lightly squeezed her other breast. Daisy began to squirm beneath him, making little mewling sounds. He continued his ministrations, bound and determined to make her ask for what she wanted.

Her knees cocked up and squeezed his hips, starting her own brand of torture.

He groaned and gave in. He sucked her nipple into his mouth.

"Yes," she moaned. "Yes, yes, yes."

Leo felt her fingers spearing through his hair, holding him close to her body. He began to pluck her other nipple, loving it when her hips arched up and her nails bit into his scalp. He needed more, so much more, but this moment of play was better than anything he'd previously experienced and he didn't want it to end.

Daisy moved again. This time it was her foot teasing the back of his leg, ever upward until it was resting on his right flank, leaving her hot, wet flesh pressed against his stomach, tempting him beyond belief.

When she started to rub herself against the ridges of his abdomen, he lost it. He literally lost it. He turned over and sat up, and grinned in satisfaction as he stared into Daisy's surprised eyes.

"I think we should try this, what do you think?"

Her hands cupped his cheeks and she swooped in for a kiss as she undulated against him. She took him ever upwards, spinning up into the heavens with her dizzying blending of lips and tongues.

As she took him over, he moved his hands along her thighs until he reached the lips of her sex. She moaned against his lips as his thumbs stroked along her silken, wet folds. Up and down, he continued to caress her, moving upwards to her clit, then he circled her swollen bud.

Daisy threw back her head and cried out.

"Leo, don't stop."

He smiled seductively. "Wasn't planning to."

He looked down where his fingers brushed against her, circling and plucking. Daisy was shaking. He caught her around her back and held her up as he continued his sexual torture. He loved watching her face as she climbed the ladder toward ecstasy.

He listened to her little cries of need, watched as her face suffused with color and her hair thrashed around her head. Nothing in his life had ever been as sexy as seeing Daisy reach for her release.

"Leo," she wailed as her hands grabbed his biceps.

"Come for me, Daisy," he said as he teased her flesh a little harder, just a little more, watching her face.

Her body shuddered, her eyes got wide, and then it hit her and she shouted out his name.

"Leo!"

"I've got you, Sweetheart."

She slumped forward and he pulled her close. For long moments, Leo did nothing more than hold her trembling body close to his, murmuring words of praise and comfort. Finally, she pushed up, her gray eyes glittering with mischief.

"Uh-oh."

"I call for a do-over."

"Are you saying you didn't like that?" Leo teased.

"Oh, you know I did, but I know a way we could both like it better."

He pushed back a stray lock of hair away from her cheek. "Daisy, listen to me, seeing you come apart in my arms, was one of the best moments of my life."

11

"Do you want to talk about what was bothering you now?" Leo asked.

Daisy couldn't understand what he was saying. Was he crazy? Hell to the no. A lady never left a gentleman wanting. At least not in her codebook.

She leaned forward and once again cupped his face. She loved the feel of his scruff against the palm of her hands. She knew she was going to have whisker burn on her breasts, and wasn't that the best? It had just added another dimension of pleasure along with his tongue and lips.

"No, Daisy, no kisses, talk," he protested. She bit his sexy lower lip and he groaned. Then she pressed her lips against his for a soft and gentle kiss. The man deserved love and care after all the beauty and bliss he had just provided to her.

Daisy felt his fingers spreading through the strands of her hair as he held her head, getting into the kiss. She scooched back a bit so that her bottom nestled his erection. He groaned into her mouth. There would be no more talking.

She began to move her hands, tracing them down the strong line of his neck, ever downward to the curls of chest hair.

Does anything feel better than this?

Daisy found his nipples and scraped her fingernails over them.

"Jesus," he groaned.

Ah, he liked that.

She pushed up and back so that she was straddling his hips and not his stomach. At long last, she was looking at his beautiful erection.

Daisy used her thumb to stroke from the bottom of his shaft to just below the head, her eyes darting between what she was doing and Leo's glittering expression. He hissed out a breath between gritted teeth.

She did it again.

And again.

Then she tried to enclose his length with one of her small hands, but it didn't quite work, so she used both hands and squeezed.

"You're killing me."

He felt so good, so much strength encased in smooth velvet, and it was hers to play with. She was in heaven. Daisy watched with interest as Leo flung out his arm and grabbed his wallet from the nightstand and wrenched out a condom.

"But I'm not done playing," she protested.

"Oh, there will be playing involved. Lots and lots of playing."

He dropped the condom by the pillow then lifted up into a sitting position.

How did he do that so easily?

He pulled her into a hug, then rolled them over so that she was lying beneath him.

Until this moment, she hadn't realized what a big man he was, and she liked it, she felt safe with him. He drew the backs of his fingers along her jaw, then bent in for a kiss. Another soul-defying, wonderous kiss, that took her into a whirlwind of sensation. He plundered her mouth, and she relished every sensation.

When he broke free, he looked down at her. "Are you absolutely sure about this?"

It took her a moment to figure out what he was asking. She turned her head slightly and caught sight of the condom in his hand. She grabbed the packet, put it to her mouth, and ripped it open.

"Now put this on."

His laughter shot through her like a sugar rush. He knelt up and applied the latex and she licked her bottom lip in anticipation.

"Lady, you are amazing."

He made her feel amazing. He made her feel wanted in a way that she never had been before. How was that even possible? Then as Leo started his slow invasion into her needy flesh she drew in an agonized breath. His eyes were staring at her face as he slowly eased his way not just into her body, but into her heart, into her soul.

As soon as those foolish thoughts entered her head she banished them, focusing instead on the feel of his cock and how good he was making her feel. She wrapped her arms around his chest, trying to seal their bodies closer together. She burrowed her face into his neck, needing to stop his penetrating gaze.

He held her, and continued to hold her, as his thrusts

met her upwards undulations. She couldn't get enough of him. When had her legs circled his waist? Was that her making those needy sounds?

She felt his hands stroking her hair and he brushed a kiss against her temple as he continued to press into her. Every stroke took her deeper into a vortex of rapture, every move drove her further into a place she'd never been before. She pulled back her head to look into his glittering brown eyes.

"There you are," he smiled.

He actually saw her. Her heart stuttered. Leo laid a gentle kiss on her lips as he continued to push her higher into the throes of pleasure. It was more than she could possibly bear.

"I don't know..."

"I've got you, Daisy. You're safe."

And with those words, she shattered into a paroxysm of pleasure, unlike anything she'd ever known before.

Somehow, even with the tidal wave of rapture, she could still hear and feel Leo's release, which catapulted her into another torrent of ecstasy.

Slowly, ever so slowly, when she came back to herself, she found herself on her side, wrapped in a loving embrace, the sight and scent of Leo surrounding her, holding back the world, keeping her safe. She snuggled even closer.

"Go to sleep, Honey. I'll be here."

And she did.

As soon as he felt her lapse into a deep sleep, Leo got up and disposed of the condom. He came back to the bed and stroked Daisy's beautiful brown hair. He pulled the sheet and duvet over her.

What in the hell had gotten her so upset?

He pulled on his pants and picked up the rest of his clothes and hers. He folded them up and put them on ottoman, then he went to sit down at Daisy's computer. He knew that whatever had upset her had to have come from a phone call or a communication from her computer. He was tempted to snoop, but he couldn't in good conscience. He needed her to tell him what had upset her so badly.

He looked back over at her and heard her give a soft snuffle. Even the sound of her snoring was dainty.

You have it bad, Perez.

God, it was only three days and he was caught up by a woman, who would have thought it? Sure as hell not his brothers and sisters, that's for damn sure. His mama would be nodding her head, saying 'of course, *mijo.*' His mom would already be planning a wedding. Leo laughed to himself. She had been trying to marry him off for the last four years; it had been killing her not to have all of her chicks married.

He got up from the desk and went into the bathroom to check his messages. The only important message was from Kane who was texting to check up on him. Yesterday had been long, and they'd only gotten about four hours' sleep before getting up at ten this morning. Then he got here by one o'clock. He sent back a brief note asking when he was needed back. Kane said tomorrow would be soon enough, which Leo appreciated.

The other messages were to be expected. But one from his sister Rosa cracked a big smile from him, seeing his niece Olivia eating her first birthday cake. It looked like she was washing her hair with the pink icing.

He quickly texted Rosa back to say how beautiful her daughter was, and how he couldn't wait to give her his gift in person. He had it stuffed in the back of his closet. It was a lamp that projected butterflies on the wall and ceiling of the nursery. This was the seventh time he'd been made an uncle, and he loved this duty and took it seriously.

He went back into the bedroom and saw that Daisy now had tried to take up all of the bed, her arms and legs splayed out. But she was such a tiny little thing, she'd still only taken up half of the bed. Leo took off his pants and folded them up and put them on the ottoman with the rest of the clothes and got into bed beside her. He pulled her in close and she immediately cuddled up. It felt good.

He started to replay what he'd seen and heard this morning, and then when he had gotten to Daisy's room. Was it possible they were connected? If she knew that her father had been beaten, it would explain Daisy's shattered mood when he had arrived, but how would she have found out?

She cuddled even closer, and the scent of orange and vanilla wafted from her hair. The smell sank into his bones. She felt so warm and soft against him, he found his mind starting to turn off and focus on the woman in his arms.

DAISY COULDN'T REMEMBER the last time she had felt so good, so unencumbered. She nuzzled Leo's neck, taking in his unique masculine scent. She wanted to remember this moment always. It was a moment out of time. How had she ever gotten this lucky? But now it was back to reality.

Now it was back to the horror that she had witnessed. She drew in a deep, shuddering breath.

"You're awake," he said softly, as his lips brushed against her temple.

"Yes," she murmured. "So are you. Do you know what time it is?"

He lifted his arm so that they could both look at the sturdy watch on his wrist. "Five p.m. Do you know how long we slept?"

"I'd say three hours if I had to guess. I wasn't really paying attention to the clock."

She rolled over so she could get a good look at him. A smile was playing on his lips, but he wasn't making fun of the situation—he looked like a man who was happy with the world. If Daisy had to guess, she had a similar expression.

"I don't mean to break the mood, but I need to go use the bathroom."

Leo grinned. "In that case, I have to break the mood too, because I'm hungry. Wanna order room service?"

She pushed up from his chest and smiled. "I like you, Leo Perez." She got out of bed and wandered over to the coffee table and grabbed the room service menu. When she spotted her sleep shirt folded up on the ottoman, she was touched. She went to grab it.

"Don't."

She looked up and saw Leo with his hands folded behind his head, leaning against the headboard.

"What?"

"Don't get dressed, at least not until you have to. You're gorgeous the way you are."

She could feel a blush starting from her chest heating

upwards to her cheeks. She walked back with the menu. "Read this, I'll be right back."

Daisy swore she could feel his eyes on her the entire time it took her to walk to the bathroom. And....she was pretty sure she liked it. By the time she got back into the bedroom, Leo was sitting up with the phone in his lap.

"What kind of food are you in the mood for?" he asked.

"Surprise me." This time she did pick up her shirt and shrug it on, then went to her suitcase to grab a fresh pair of panties.

"Hey, I thought we had a deal," he griped.

"I've got to see what the e-mail fairy gifted me with, and I refuse to sit naked on the chair, it just seems wrong."

Daisy tuned Leo out while he was ordering and focused on the forty-three new e-mails that had come in since she'd last checked. She forced herself not to think of the video that she had seen. After years of practice, she was pretty good at compartmentalizing, and she would use that skill now.

"Shit."

"What?" Leo asked.

"Oh, it's nothing new. Just more roadblocks on one of the schools we're trying to open in Cambodia. The government's only happy if they get their beak wet."

"Is that something you can handle now?"

She shook her head. "It goes to Reggie. Chanlina was just telling me because she still doesn't feel comfortable talking to men. I'm going to have to send Reggie to Phnom Penh for a month or so, then she can see what a good guy he is."

She jumped when there was a knock on the door.

"Why don't you hit the bathroom and I let in the server?" Leo suggested.

It made sense, and she really appreciated it, so she nodded. When she went into the bathroom, she took a good look at herself and laughed. Never had her hair looked so eighties girl-band before. She definitely was sporting sex hair.

She got out her brush and went about taming it. When she was done she looked down at the spot where she had been curled up in front of the toilet this morning and bit her lip. An overwhelming wave of anguish hit her as she thought of her dad. She had to grip the sink to continue to stay standing.

"Are you all right in there?"

"Huh?"

"I thought I heard you cry out. Are you okay, Daisy?"

She looked at herself in the mirror and realized she really wasn't okay.

12

LEO KNOCKED AGAIN AND DAISY OPENED THE BATHROOM door just as he was going to knock once more. She was not the same woman who had gone into the bathroom. Something had happened.

"What's wrong?"

She just shook her head and moved past him, careful not to touch him. Yep, something was way wrong. Once again she looked like the woman he had walked in on hours ago. This time he was going to get to the bottom of things.

"I'm going to put some clothes on real quick, then we can eat."

"Okay," he said slowly. He watched as she grabbed something from her suitcase then went back to the bathroom. This he could understand; after all, he was back in his clothes. In a Muslim country, he wasn't about to open the door in just his pants, of course he had put on his shirt.

She came back out in yoga pants and a peach

sleeveless blouse that fell past her hips. Her expression was stoic.

"I think you need some food." He sat her down at the small couch in front of the coffee table and whipped off the lids from the food. He hadn't ordered Western food—it was always such a crapshoot in other countries, it was best to stick with native dishes.

Daisy gave a wan smile even when he unveiled *badenjan borani* to start.

"Oh Daisy, there must be something really wrong if this isn't doing it for you. It's eggplant simmered in tomato sauce with garlic yogurt. I thought this would really turn your crank."

She let out a half-hearted laugh.

He put the lid back over the dish and sat down beside her. "Can you tell me what's wrong?"

"It's Dad," she whispered.

"Alistair?"

She shook her head. "Ethan. My biological dad. I saw something horrible."

Ah fuck. She's seen the video.

"Do you want to tell me?"

She looked up at him, her eyes filled with tears.

"Yes. No. I don't know."

He scooched closer and grabbed her hand. "You saw a video, didn't you?"

She put her other hand on top of his and nodded her head. "How did you know? Did someone tell you about it? Did you see it?"

A tear dripped down her face. She swiped it away by wiping her cheek onto her shoulder.

"Yes, I saw it."

"They hurt him so bad. They want to kill him, Leo."

That was the point when he realized that she hadn't really—hadn't consciously—figured that out yet. She might have talked a good game, but this was the first time it had settled in for her that her father was going to be murdered. He thought back to their talk at lunch, the way she seemed to compartmentalize her feelings, especially when it came to Ethan.

"I know, Daisy."

"I don't want him to die," her voice was forlorn.

"I know you don't."

"What am I going to do? How am I going to save him?" Her hands clenched his.

"Honey, you're not. You can't. What you're going to do is let the professionals handle it."

"But that's not what I do. I always help."

God, she's killing me.

He wrapped his arms around her and she fell against his chest. She didn't cry, but her body heaved dry sobs against him.

"But what if you can't rescue him?"

"We can. It's what we do."

Jesus, did I just make that promise? Stupid, Perez. Really goddamn stupid.

She looked up at him, her eyes shimmering with tears. "I know you'll try. But I don't want you hurt, either." Her hands gripped his shirt, her nails biting into his chest.

"Daisy, how did you get ahold of that video? Who gave it to you?"

She looked away. "I can't tell you."

"You have to. Not only is it important from a security standpoint, but whoever showed you that video is not a friend of yours."

"How can you say that? I needed to know what was

going on with my father. Leo, you should have seen it. It was horrible."

"Daisy, I did see it," he admitted. "That's why I'm saying whoever showed it to you isn't a friend of yours. Think about it—would you ever show a family member something like that? Ever?"

He watched her wheels turn.

"*Ever*, Daisy. You would tell them about it, and say that their father was alive, but you wouldn't show it to them, right? What kind of person would show that to you?"

"He's a good man," she protested. But Leo could see that his words had gotten through.

"Fine, he's a good man. Tell me who he is. It was hard enough for our men to get our guys to find this, but how did your guy come across it?"

She let go of his shirt and tried to sit back, but Leo wasn't having any of it. She was staying where she belonged, in his arms. "I don't know his sources. He's a reporter. I don't think he would ever tell anybody how he got his hands on that video. But Alistair has worked with him in the past. He vouches for him, so that's good enough in my book."

"Fine. But give me a name. If he has this kind of info, he might have something else that would help us. I know that your natural inclination is to keep this to yourself and try to come up with your 'back-up' plan, but Daisy, you need to rely on us now. Hopefully, you see that."

He could see the conflict in her eyes. She was such a capable and strong woman. She reminded him of all the strong and capable women in his family, but she was someone whose trust had been badly broken by different people. He waited for her to make a decision. Finally, she nodded.

"Rayi Abad. He's an Afghan reporter. He's been smuggling out reports for years under different bylines."

"Do you have a way to contact him?"

"He has only Skype'd me. So that's the only incoming communication I've received from him. My stepfather has something, but I'm not sure he would give it to me."

"Can I see the Skype address he used?"

Daisy nodded. She got up from the couch and Leo followed her to the desk. She pulled up the Skype conversation. Leo used the hotel stationery to write out Rayi's Skype address. "I'm going to call my computer expert and let him work with this while you eat something, is it a deal?"

She shook her head.

Leo frowned. "What do you mean, no?"

"You have to eat, too."

He laughed. "I will. Just let me make this call, then I will be eating right beside you."

She let out a sigh of relief as she went back over to the coffee table. She started lifting lids off the plates.

"You did a good job choosing food. Thank you." Her smile was half-hearted at best, still, it was something.

"I'm glad you like it. I'm just going to step out in the hall for a minute."

She opened her mouth to ask a question, then closed it and nodded.

Leo went out in the hall and walked down to the end of the corridor to make his call.

"Kane, have some info."

"Give it to me."

"Reporter by the name of Rayi Abad sent Daisy the video that we saw this morning of her father being beaten." Leo watched the hallway that led to the elevators, making sure no one came out of them.

"Shit, why the hell would someone do that?" Kane bit out.

"That's my question. Anyway, he did. I want to know where he got the info and what his real motive was behind sending it to Daisy. He could have just told her he'd seen a video of her father or sent her a picture from the video, he didn't need to send her the whole thing."

"You're right on the money, Leo. Did she give you any contact information on this guy?"

"I've got his Skype address. Can you find him from that?"

There was dead silence.

Leo laughed. "I'm so sorry I doubted your expertise, oh great computer genius."

"There you go," Kane chuckled. "Now give me his address and I shall work my magic. You *are* still coming back tonight, right?"

"That's the plan, why?"

"Captain Miller came up with more info that looks somewhat promising. It's thirty klicks from where we were last night."

"What did she find?" Leo straightened up.

"Dogs outside a cave. No jeep, no truck. But the cave has a wide entrance; according to Miller this wouldn't be the first time that vehicles were hidden in the caves."

"Are we going in?" Leo asked.

"She's been doing drone flyovers for the last four hours. She's going to continue for another four and report back to us. If it looks promising, we'll take another ride with Wilma tonight."

"Gotcha."

IT FELT cold in the hotel room. She couldn't tell if it was because Leo had turned up the AC before they'd made love, or because he'd left—either way, she was cold. Daisy got up and adjusted the temperature then she drew back the sheers to let in more sun. She stood by the window, basking in the warmth as she thought about Leo's words.

No matter what angle she looked at, she couldn't find any upside for Rayi to upset her with the video. Yeah, what Leo said made sense—that he could have been kinder and just told her that her father was alive instead of sending her the file, but she would have demanded proof. Rayi would have known that, so wasn't he just being expedient?

Now that she had her head pulled out of her ass and could think rationally, she realized that Leo and his team were her father's best bet. It killed her to admit it. Knowing that she didn't have any power in a situation was anathema for her.

With the first knock on the door, she hurried over to let Leo in.

"This is the second time you didn't use the peephole or use the chain on the door. You need to be more safety-conscious."

"Both times I knew it was you."

"Use the guard chain, check the peephole, I don't care how sure you are. Use them."

He was right, she would counsel another woman to do the same thing. "You're right. I promise to do that next time. Now come and eat, the food is getting cold."

She sat down in the same place she had been and was

happy when Leo took his same spot, even though it was clear she was past the point of needing comforting.

"I ordered four different dishes so we could serve ourselves family-style."

"Who else are you inviting over?"

"You need to eat a decent amount of food. Plus there's me. I'm a growing boy." He winked at her.

There was something about that wink. That humor. That man.

Daisy smiled. A real smile. Not a sex-satisfied smile, not that those hadn't been tremendously wonderful. Nope, this was a smile that said maybe time with this man, and believing in him, in his capabilities, might just work out.

"Why aren't you filling your plate? I thought you said you liked what I'd ordered."

"I do. I was thinking how much I like you."

Leo coughed on the kebab he was eating. "Daisy, I sure as hell hope you kind of liked me before we hit the sheets."

"There you go again, that's another reason I like you, you have a great sense of humor. I do, I really do like you." She looked at the stubble on his face, and the white gleam of his smile, and felt like she'd hit the proverbial jackpot.

"Are you going to pass me a note? Should I be careful that my lieutenant doesn't see it?"

"You goofball."

He pulled the empty plate out of her hand and started to fill it up.

"I could have done that."

"But you weren't."

She noticed how he filled it with primarily vegetarian

items. "Do you want any of the meat dishes?" he finally asked.

"Chicken," she nodded.

He spooned some of the *narenj palaw* onto her plate. He seriously chose some good dishes. When her dish was full, she sat back and started to eat.

"You don't have to watch me," she complained. "I will finish my meal."

"Maybe I just enjoy watching you eat."

Daisy watched as he took a bite of his lamb dumplings. He was right, there was something sensual about watching a person eat. Just seeing how his lips closed around the tongs of his fork made her want to kiss him. Or better yet, have him take a bite out of her.

Cool it. I'm eating dinner, not getting ready to jump the man!

"I thought about what you said, but I can't figure out any sort of angle where it would behoove Rayi to show me that video out of spite. He knows who I am, what I do. He realized I could handle it, and Leo? I should have. I can't believe I broke down like that."

He gave her a sideways look. "Are you in the habit of lying to yourself? I'm just curious."

She took another bite of her chicken dish and noticed that this time it tasted like sawdust. She put down her plate. "In all reality, I didn't think it would affect me. So no, I'm not lying to myself. I didn't know that seeing my biological dad in so much pain...realizing that he's going to be executed, was going to..." She gulped in a deep breath, then continued. "Well, I just didn't know it would affect me so strongly. I didn't realize how deep a connection I had to him. Part of the reason I wanted to be the one to come over here, instead of my brothers and sister, is I could handle it if something bad were to happen because I would be less attached. This sure blew my thought process all to hell, huh?"

"You do realize it only proves you're a deeply compassionate and loving woman."

"Who probably should have listened to her mother when she was fifteen." Daisy waved her hand in the air. "Okay, enough about my Daddy issues. What did you and your teammate talk about? I know you can't tell me much of anything, but can you tell me something?"

"I have to go back to Bagram Air Base early this evening, I can tell you that. I can also tell you that my teammate is checking into Rayi, but other than that, nothing."

"And Jim's Russian connection?"

"I brought that to Tom's attention yesterday. That should be the end of things."

Daisy felt a big sense of relief. At least that was done.

"And how early is early?"

Leo looked at his watch. "I probably have to leave here in the next forty-five minutes."

"I'm done eating, what about you?"

"Depends," Leo smiled at her. "Do you have an activity that is more enticing than eating in mind?"

"I think I do. I really think I do."

13

This time the Blackhawk couldn't land anywhere close to the cave; there just wasn't the kind of terrain coverage to hide behind. As well as not having the mountainous area for coverage, there was not going to be any high ground for Leo and Ezio to set up good sniper positions. Which sucked—really, really sucked.

Hell, Leo didn't mind the twenty-klick hike from the Blackhawk to the cave with the sixty pounds of gear. That was a cakewalk, but not having a good position to cover his teammates? Yeah, that really chapped his hide. That's not to say he and Ezio hadn't come up with a plan. The drone footage had shown some rock groupings and formations that looked promising, but they wouldn't know until they got closer.

"Hold up," Max said over their comm system.

They could see the cliff in the distance. Max had his night-vision binoculars out, and soon everybody else did as well.

"I'm seeing three perfect hidey-holes on that cliff above the cave for sentries," Raiden said with disgust.

"I only saw two," Asher said. "Where's the third?"

"Did you see the one right above the cave, dead center? It almost blends in with the mouth of the cave, so you don't really notice it, but it's a crease in the rock," Raiden explained. "I don't see anyone in there, but I'd bet my bottom dollar someone with a rifle has wormed their way back in there."

"Got it," Asher answered.

"Ezio and Leo. There's your first order of business—take those guys out before we get into range. Can you do it?"

Leo looked over at Ezio and grinned. "Absolutely, Boss."

Leo never used binoculars, not when he had the best rifle scope in the world, so he pulled his out while Ezio was doing the same thing. Without any discussion, they started determining where they could set up shop.

"I'll take the one on the right, four klicks ahead," Leo said.

"I'm on the left, four klicks and a few meters past that one," Ezio stated.

"Men. Stay behind our snipers. After they get into position, I'll give the go-ahead to move forward." Max didn't bother looking at each man, he knew they would do exactly what he said.

Now that they had their targets they moved faster. Soon Leo was at his rock formation. He scrambled up and had his rifle set up in no time. Raiden had been right, of course; Leo could see hands gripping an AK-47 through the crevice. That was it, but it was enough.

Leo waited until Ezio was in position as he scoured around the cave for any other potential spots where lookouts might be hiding. His rifle moved infinitesimally as he caught sight of movement inside the cave. He adjusted his scope a little more and saw two men huddled together near the mouth of the cave in some kind of in-depth conversation. *Not smart, they should not be that close to the entrance. Lucky us.*

Leo took a glance and saw that Ezio was set up. "You seeing what I'm seeing, Stark?" he asked his teammate. "I've got five—two inside the cave, three hiding above the cave."

"I count the same," Ezio concurred.

There was a cluster of trees a klick to the right of the cave. Coming from that angle would be the best, but they would have to veer at least seven kilometers out of their way to get there. It would require Max and the team another seven miles of hiking to avoid the open plain in front of the cave, and come at them from the trees.

Before Leo could say anything, Max was up on the rock formation with him. "Whatchya got?"

Leo handed over his rifle so Max could see what he had been seeing. "So coming at them from the left, through the trees is the best plan of attack," Max said.

"Yeah, but it's going to mean we start our attack at zero four hundred not zero three hundred." Leo sighed.

Max and Leo looked at one another. They both knew that zero three hundred was the best time for an attack; the closer they got to dawn, the better chance that the men in the cave would be active.

"No choice." Max handed the rifle back to Leo and jumped down from the perch.

"You're in luck," he whispered into his mic to the rest of the team. "We get more exercise. About seven more kilometers to go, instead of one."

"Cool, I think I've been putting on weight." Cullen laughed at his own joke.

"I've noticed," Max said. "I want you to carry my pack."

Cullen stopped laughing.

Leo watched as they all started off. Even though he was ninety-nine point nine percent sure they wouldn't be noticed, he still kept watch on the Afghan look-outs to make sure they didn't make any funny moves. Leo took it as his personal mission to keep his team alive.

Leo couldn't explain how time worked during situations like these; it was like it slowed down to an absolute crawl and sped to warp speed. He continued to watch and saw the AK-47 change hands. He saw a third man join the other two at the mouth of the cave. Then he saw the man sitting cross-legged near the top of the cliff start to drift off to sleep.

At the same time, he watched each member of his team move closer and closer to the trees. Even from his place on the rocks, little movements made it easy for him to determine who was who. Kane would occasionally reach back and touch his backpack that held his 'precious' laptop. Max took the rear to watch over his chicks, while Raiden took point. Nic would occasionally speed up and then slow down, always anxious to get to where he was going. Asher never missed a step, calm cool, and collected, steady as always. Then there was Cullen, moving back and forth between the men, checking up on everyone. Yep, that was his team.

"Do you see that?" Ezio whispered.

"Yep," Leo answered. "He's just looking, I don't think he sees anything," Leo said referring to the man who had been on his stomach, hidden partly behind a bush on the cliff. He was now up on his knees with his rifle held to his shoulder. But he wasn't aiming at Max and the team, he was pointed at Ezio and Leo. Leo wasn't worried, neither they nor their rifles were observable from the cliff. *The man must just have a gut feeling or is checking things out.*

Leo didn't move a muscle and he knew that Ezio wasn't either. Finally, the man went back to a prone position. When Leo felt good enough again, he peeked over at his team and saw they had made it damn near another klick. They were almost at the trees. It wasn't until they left on the other side that things would get *interesting.* It was three forty-five. Leo hissed in a breath. They were cutting things really fucking close.

When a fourth man joined the three at the mouth of the cave Leo was using every swear word he knew, in every language he knew. *Is everybody in the cave awake!?* He watched as the fourth man said something that caused the others to laugh, then they all shushed themselves and peered around as if to make sure nobody had heard them. Good, maybe not everybody was awake.

"Four at the front of the cave to the far left, shooting the shit. Still just the three lookouts, one is asleep," Leo said into his mic.

"Gotcha," Max responded. "We're heading in."

Even though Leo knew to be looking for them, they were hard to detect, as each member of his team moved slow and low out of the line of trees. They went the twenty meters to the cliff and hung close to the side as they crept along the mouth of the cave that was wide enough to drive two trucks through side by side. God only knew how big and deep the cave itself was.

Leo did a headcount—all six were there, and they would be ghosts inside the cave. First, they had to get past the four—nope, make that three—men who were still talking. The jokester had left.

"Only three men at the mouth of the cave now," Ezio reported.

All six men slipped into the cave one after the other, unnoticed by the three men who were still talking away. There was no movement from the lookouts because they were still focused on the terrain in front of the cave, not straight down the side of the cliff.

Leo waited for thirteen heartbeats after his team was in the cave, then watched as each of the three terrorists who had been talking were taken from behind, their mouths covered as a knife silently dispatched their lives.

The longer the team could go without using their guns, the better off they were.

Leo jerked ever so slightly as he heard the first gunshots being fired from an assault rifle. *So much for silence.* Leo took out the guy right above the cave. He heard Ezio fire. Leo had his rifle trained on the man who had just woken up, and he killed him. All the while, he heard screams and loud spurts of assault fire over his receiver.

"Fuck!"

"Goddammit!"

It was Cullen and Nic. Had they been shot?

He saw headlights at almost the same instant as his teammates had started cursing. It had probably blinded them in their goggles. An engine roared to life. More rifle fire continued in the cave.

He heard a grunt of pain come over his receiver. It was one of their team, but who?

Leo didn't have time to give a shit, they had bigger fish to fry as a truck with a canvas covering on the back came barreling out of the cave and headed toward Ezio and Leo's hiding spots.

"No doctor," Max said over his mic. "He could be in the truck."

"Gotcha," Ezio responded.

"Tires," Leo told Ezio.

"Agreed." They didn't want to take out the driver for fear of an immediate wreck, so they'd go for the tires to begin with.

"Left side," Ezio said.

"Right side," Leo responded.

Shooting out all of the tires at once was the best way to ensure the truck didn't end up on its side or upend itself. Leo spotted a driver and someone in the passenger seat. With the back covered, they had no idea how many were in the back.

As the truck got closer, Leo called out, "Now."

They took their shots and the tires exploded. The driver kept driving. It was going slow. Perfect time to take out the people in the front seat. Leo took out the driver and Ezio took out the one in the passenger seat. The truck was closest to Leo. He jumped down off his rock, leaving his sniper rifle and pulling his M4 assault rifle off his back. He kept it in front of him as he moved in to see what he was dealing with in the back of the truck.

In the distance, he saw one man running toward him from the cave. "Coming your way," Nic said.

"On the other side," Ezio breathed into the mic.

"On the count of three," Leo said as softly.

They came around the opposite sides and threw back the sides of the canvas tarp. Four men were in the back. Two were obviously unconscious but were held up anyway, as human shields. One had a gun to his head, the other a knife to his throat.

The one who held the knife screamed in Dari, "I'll kill him."

He was holding Daisy's father.

Leo had no doubt in his mind that he was willing to kill his hostage.

"Siraj Haqqani will not be happy if you kill him without his permission," Leo said calmly in Dari.

The man's eyes widened. "What do you know of him?"

"I know that he would kill you *and* your family if you were to take the life of the doctor without his permission."

"You will kill me anyway, so what's the point?"

"I promise not to kill you. You and your friend release your hostages, and you will be taken alive."

Leo saw him considering his words. He whispered to the other man, who shook his head vehemently. But the man with the knife continued to talk. Leo could hear him talking about their families. Finally, the man with the gun let his arm drop. It was enough; Ezio and Leo jumped into the truck and rushed the men.

The Haqqani terrorists dropped their unconscious prisoners and held up their hands. "Max," Leo called into his mic. "We've got the doc and the reporter."

"We've got the place cleared out here," Kane answered. "I'm calling Wilma to touch down here."

"Was someone injured?" Ezio asked.

"Yeah," Raiden answered. "It was Cullen bitching and whining about a flesh wound."

"I wasn't complaining about the wound, I was complaining about the way you doctored me up." Leo could hear the grimace in Cullen's voice. It was obviously worse than a flesh wound.

Leo would bet his bottom dollar that Raiden had stayed close to Cullen because he'd had one of his feelings. He was weird that way. Kind of like Kane was about his magic with computers.

"Kane, tell Wilma it's going to be packed, that we have two prisoners we're bringing aboard," Ezio said.

"Got it."

14

It was the ambassador who called her. Funny, Daisy had been expecting to hear from Leo.

"Your father has been rescued, Miss Squires. He's at the hospital at Bagram Air Base."

Her level of relief took her by surprise, but she didn't have time to process it. "I'll be there as soon as possible," she said. She started looking around her hotel room for her purse.

"No, he has to be debriefed. You won't be able to visit him for a couple of days. I just wanted to let you know he's safe. We've already called your brother in the states."

"What in the hell do you mean I can't visit him right now, that's utter bullshit." Daisy kept the phone to her ear as she grabbed her purse and looked for her shoes. She looked in the hotel mirror and frowned.

She'd have to change; the sweatpants wouldn't work.

"Miss Squires, I'll try to expedite the debriefing process so you can see him sooner, but protocol needs to be observed."

"I understand. Thank you for the call." She hung up and called Malek.

"Malek?"

"Yes, ma'am." Daisy winced. She couldn't break him of that habit.

"Could I get a ride to Bagram? They rescued my father and he's at the hospital there at the Air Base."

"I can't, ma'am, but my nephew can. I can send him to your hotel immediately."

"That would be great."

While she was talking to him, she grabbed a skirt and blouse out of the closet.

This will work.

She got dressed in record time, even had time to brush her hair and pee, before the hour-and-a-half trip to Bagram Air Force Base. She went down to the lobby and waited outside in the heat near the valet. They looked at her weirdly.

"Can I help you, ma'am?"

"I'm waiting for my ride," she assured him.

"The hotel offers a driver for our guests."

Malek's nephew pulled up at that moment. The valet looked disapprovingly at his car. She didn't care. When she went to open the door, the valet still opened it for her.

"My uncle said that you are in a hurry. Do we have to worry about people following you?" the young man asked eagerly.

"No, not this time." At least she hoped not.

"Oh." He was obviously disappointed. It still didn't stop him from driving like a bat out of hell when they pulled into the Kabul traffic. Once again Daisy found herself clutching the St. Christopher medal. When they got onto the highway to Bagram, she sighed a breath of relief.

"Is your father well?" the young man asked.

"I know he's safe," Daisy answered. "I don't know how injured he is. That's why I'm going to the hospital."

"I shall pray for him."

"Thank you," Daisy said sincerely.

It took them an hour and twelve minutes to get to the base, but then it took them twenty minutes to be let through the front gate. She had to invoke the name of Leo Perez. The first thirteen times they said they had never heard of him.

The fourteenth time was the charm.

Malek's nephew was directed to park outside a rather small building that she assumed was the hospital since someone was wheeling a person out in a wheelchair. She was opening the backseat door when the other backseat door opened and Leo slid in beside her.

"You shouldn't be here," he said.

Was he seriously going to try and stop her from going into the hospital? *Has he met me?* "Not you too."

"I'm serious, Daisy. He's alive. But the brass and suits have to talk to him. Then there are people like us who need to find out everything they can about where he's been so we might be able to help others one day."

"Why can't they do that after I spend ten minutes with him?" she asked. "And another thing. Why didn't you answer one single phone call or text? Why did the guard at the front gate pretend you didn't exist? What the hell, Leo?" All her feelings of abandonment came roaring up, but not hard enough that she couldn't push them back down again.

Mostly.

"While I'm in-country, and until the mission is completed, that's what I needed to do. I'm flying out of here in less than an hour. I swear to you, I'm going to call you as soon as I hit American soil."

"Oh really, and I'm supposed to believe this why?" Now she was getting pretty fucking angry.

"We promised no lies. Have I lied to you yet?" he asked softly.

"You ignored me. You ghosted me. You left me in the dark. Think about how that made me feel."

"We were supposed to be wheels-up four hours ago. I was not allowed to tell you that your father had been found or have any contact with you. But all bets are off when I'm home."

She looked into his warm brown eyes that were willing her to believe. He was, he was *willing* her to believe him. Daisy hadn't had much dealing with the military, but maybe this was the way it worked.

He reached for her hand and held it tightly. "Please," he said.

Her jaw clenched. She didn't have time to wonder if this was just another empty promise despite Leo's honesty. She needed to get in to see her father. If she agreed, maybe he'd back off.

Daisy nodded.

"You need to leave," he said.

"Oh hell no. You have your part to play. I understand that. So, I never saw you. I get that. Maybe I'll hear from you, maybe I won't."

His face became stony. "You will. Take that to the bank."

"Whatever." But her heart was bleeding. "But I get it, this talk isn't taking place right now. So, get the hell out of the car. I'm going to play my part, which is I'm going to storm the hospital and rattle some cages until they have no choice but let this troublesome woman see my dad."

"Daisy—"

"Leave, Leo."

He looked over at Malek's nephew, then grabbed her clenched hand and pulled it open. He brought her palm to his mouth and kissed it. She closed her eyes.

Please, please, please God, let him call me. He sees me.

"Go, Leo."

He slid out of the car as silently as he had come into it. She blinked back tears. Then she got out on her side, her purse over her arm. Ready for battle.

————

SHE HADN'T SEEN Ethan Squires for five years, and he didn't look like the man she remembered. He'd aged twenty years, and it wasn't just the bruises. It was the wrinkles and the gray hair she hadn't noticed in the video.

"Dad? Can you hear me?"

"We sedated him two hours ago. He was getting pretty agitated."

"When will he wake up?" Daisy asked the doctor.

"Probably in another three hours."

"I suppose that's when the welcome party is due back to question him some more?" she deduced.

"Actually I told them that he would sleep through the night," the doctor told her with a twinkle in his eye.

What a wonderful man. For the first time since entering the hospital room, Daisy smiled.

"Can I sit with him until he wakes up?"

"When was the last time you've eaten? We serve a mean grilled cheese sandwich."

"Tomato soup?" Daisy asked.

"Of course."

Daisy sank down in the plastic chair and gave the doctor a wan smile. "Who do I have to kill?"

"I think we can save you from a murder charge. I'll have it sent over. Your dad's going to be okay. We're more worried about Dick Summers."

Daisy frowned. Where had she heard that name before? Then she realized that was the reporter who had been kidnapped months before. "He was rescued too? That's wonderful," she grinned. Then she looked at the doctor. "Wait a minute, are you saying he might not make it?"

"Yes, he's going to make it. Sorry, I shouldn't have said what I did. But yes, he should make it. I'm really tired. It's been a long night."

"Perhaps you need a grilled cheese before heading to bed," Daisy suggested.

"Perhaps you're right," the doctor agreed. "Anyway, you stay here with your father. He's going to be fine. He'll be glad you're here."

"I hope so," Daisy said with a frown.

"I know so."

———

DAISY WAS in the midst of answering her e-mails on her phone when she heard her dad's breathing change. She looked up and saw him watching her.

"Daisy?"

She got up and stood over his bed.

"Yeah, it's me, Dad." She grabbed his hand and he hung on tightly.

"How'd you get here?"

"It's a long story. How are you feeling?"

"Like someone beat the hell out of me." His laughter ended in a coughing fit. Daisy raised his bed and grabbed the glass of water by his bed.

"Here, drink slowly."

He tried to hold the glass in his hands but they were too shaky. She helped him. Four sips later, and he'd stopped coughing.

She saw his eyes well up with tears.

"Dad, it's going to be all right. You're safe now."

His lips tightened, and he nodded.

"Can I get you something? Food maybe? They have a really good grilled cheese and tomato soup."

"No, just having you here means everything to me."

His words threatened to open her up so she deflected. "How did this happen? What happened?" she asked.

"Baby, I don't want to talk about it right now, okay? I have more than enough people asking that. Hell, they want to know my shoe size and I swear to God they'd really like to perform a colonoscopy on me if they could. So no questions about that, okay?"

"Sure, Dad."

"I like hearing that," he said softly.

Shit. This emotional shit is a lot to handle.

"Yeah, well..."

"It's okay, I won't always expect it. Just hearing it now is enough."

She nodded.

Damn it, am I tearing up?

"You have some really determined children. They

were getting senators involved to pressure the State Department to get you released."

"But you're the one over here." Again he squeezed her hand.

"They just knew I was the ballbuster of the family. They figured if anyone could knock some heads I'd be the one who could do it."

His lip twitched. "You were like that even at two years old. Your terrible twos were awful. Once you learned the word 'no', your mother and I were in hell."

"Like you were around," Daisy said. Then she immediately regretted the words.

"Oh, there were a couple of years I was there. You can ask your mother. I knew you would set the world on fire one day, and you have."

"Look, you don't have to be handing out the compliments. I'm here. I'm not going anywhere."

He closed his eyes, then opened them. "Fair enough. Tell me more about Jim, Brian, and Karen."

"First, are you hungry?"

"I couldn't keep anything down. I'd just like it if you'd talk."

Daisy nodded and pulled up the chair.

15

"WHAT CRAWLED UP YOUR ASS?" CULLEN ASKED. "I'M THE one who's going to have to explain to my wife that I let myself get injured. She's going to be pissed."

Leo looked down at the same page he'd been staring at for the last hour, ignoring Cullen. They'd been on the transport plane for five hours, and for three of them, members of the team had tried to engage him in conversation. Everybody but Max. He knew better.

Max had known that Daisy would be pressuring Leo for information about her father, and Leo would have to keep his mouth shut. That meant that he couldn't have contact with her. It killed him. He knew proper channels were going to inform her that her father was fine, but she wouldn't be able to see him for a while, which would go over like a lead balloon.

He should have known she'd push like a pit bull. And he'd admired the hell out of her. But he hated the hell out of it when she'd turned that fierce fire on him. He'd wished she'd just believed in him, but he'd known. He'd *known* why she couldn't have faith. After so many broken promises in her life, it was going to be up to him to take the time to help her build that trust.

"You haven't turned a page for at least an hour. Come on, talk to me. I'm a great listener," Cullen coaxed.

Leo snorted. "You're a great talker, is what you are."

"See, same thing. You listen, I talk. What's the difference? You need a good talking-to."

"Oh really?" Leo said sarcastically. "Just what sort of advice are you going to give me?"

"Well, it's easy. You don't have job worries. You don't live above your means. Your family couldn't be any more perfect. So it's woman troubles. Since you were fine before the mission, then you had to go get info from Ms. Squires —who I Googled, by the way—she's your problem. How am I doing so far?"

Shit, shit, shit. Why didn't they hire stupid men to become SEALs?

"You might have hit on something, but maybe I'm just worried about her because they're not reuniting her with her father right away."

"Sure...that's what has your dick in a twist. I believe you." Cullen clearly didn't.

Leo looked around the transport plane to see who else was listening in on their conversation. It was really loud in the back of the plane, but then so was Cullen Lyons. He saw Raiden with a half-smile on his face beside Cullen. But, hell, he didn't mind if Raiden knew his business; he kept his own counsel.

"Yes, it's Daisy," he admitted slowly. "And what the hell is up with us meeting women on missions? That's just plain wrong."

Cullen chuckled, then winced.

"Serves you right," Leo laughed. He knew that Cullen had gotten cut with a knife along his side, not deep enough to need surgery, but enough that he'd ended up with a fuck ton of stitches.

"Hey, be nice to the wounded. I'm being nice to the lovelorn. I'm going to give you advice and everything."

"Okay, I'll bite, what's the advice?"

"Grovel."

Leo sat up straighter. This had the ring of truth. "I'm listening."

"I don't know what happened, but assume it is your fault, and grovel."

"It is my fault," Leo said quietly. "I had to leave. I ghosted her calls because I knew she'd push me for information on her father that I couldn't answer. Then when she showed up at the base, I told her she needed to leave. I promised her I would call her when I was stateside, but she didn't believe me."

"This is bad, Dude. Groveling isn't going to be enough. Flowers sure as hell won't cut it. You're going to have to track her down when we get home and grovel in person. Take her out."

"She's not going to want to see me."

"Where's that Perez charm? You usually have to shake them off with a stick."

"Daisy's different."

"They always are when they're important. Anyway, you're going to have to figure out a way for the two of you to talk. You can do this. Then you grovel. Take it from a man who knows, this works."

Raiden snorted.

Cullen turned to him. "Wait until it's your turn."

Again, Raiden just smiled and shook his head. Then he leaned forward. "I wish you luck, Perez."

"I'll take it."

16

I<small>T WAS WORSE THAN SHE</small>'<small>D BEEN TOLD</small>. I<small>T WAS ALWAYS</small>
worse. The little girl held her hand for all she was worth,
which wasn't much. Daisy could tell that she didn't have
much strength. It was obvious she was tired and
undernourished. She was pulling Daisy toward her home
within the internally displaced person camp here in
Aden, the fourth largest city in Yemen.

"Come, come. You will meet my mother and brothers
and sisters and cousins." Abia had been talking non-stop
in Arabic since Daisy had first met her. Daisy was only
understanding every third word, but it was enough. She
realized that there was only her mother, no father, no
aunts or uncles. This was exactly the type of woman she
wanted to talk to.

The girl looked maybe three years old, but the aid
worker explained she was extremely malnourished and
was in fact five years old. There was a lot of good work
being done by some of the different international aid
organizations here in Yemen, but it was like trying to stop
a flood with a finger in a dam, it wasn't doing a damn

thing. Daisy was here to specifically evaluate the plight of the Yemeni women. She knew the statistics—one out of every four displaced families was headed by a woman or a girl. The girls were often looking to marry, often times a much older man, just to feed their younger siblings.

"We must hurry, Miss," the girl said for the tenth time, but it was her little body that was slowing them down. Daisy couldn't stand it another minute. She bent and scooped her up.

"Abia, why don't you just point me in the right direction? My legs are longer, this will be really fast. I promise," Daisy said slowly in Arabic, hoping she got the pronunciation correct.

The little girl looked up at her with assessing brown eyes. Her body might look like a baby's but her eyes were that of an adult. Finally, Abia nodded. She relaxed against Daisy and pointed. "That way."

How the child could determine which way to go was a mystery to Daisy, since all the tents looked the same to her, but the girl was steadfast. She continued to lead Daisy down different rows of tents until she finally screeched, "This one!"

She scrambled to get down from Daisy's arms.

Abia scurried into the tent, leaving Daisy outside waiting. There was no way she was going to enter without an invite. She heard a lot of talking inside. Many people walked past her, looking at her curiously in her Western garb. She smiled and wished them well.

The canvas door of the tent was brushed aside and a woman was staring at Daisy suspiciously, Abia by her side. "Hello. What do you want?" she asked. She was just this side of rude. Apparently, Westerners had not been her friend over the years.

"I'm here to ask you some questions, and see if I could help you."

"How?"

Daisy dropped down to a crouch and undid her backpack. She pulled out a one-gallon plastic jug of water. The woman's eyes went wide with avarice. Daisy handed it to her. Then she pulled out twenty packets of the surprisingly tasty, protein-rich peanut butter paste that had been a Godsend for those countries enduring famine. The woman's eyes teared up.

"May I come in?" Daisy asked as Abia grabbed for the peanut butter packs.

"My name is Maysa," the woman said as she opened the tent door further. Inside it was bright, and Daisy could easily see at least eight other children sitting around. Three of them were coloring in coloring books. Two were listless, lying on blankets. Maysa called to the two oldest, a boy and a girl, to come and get the jug of water. The others stared at Daisy.

"How can I help you?" Maysa asked. She pointed to a spot on the dirt floor with a precious rug on it.

Daisy watched as the water and peanut butter packs were carefully put in a box. Not one child made a play for the contents, instead respecting that they would get something later. Maysa had taught them restraint, which was amazing considering the circumstances.

"I'm here trying to better understand the specific needs of the Yemeni women. I need someone who can help me better understand what it's like to be the head of the household for more than your own family."

"These children are my family. Some I gave birth to, some are my brother's children. But they are all my family," Maysa said with quiet dignity.

Daisy bowed her head in apology. "I am sorry. Of course, you are right."

"There are other women who have taken in their neighbors' children after their parents have died. They too, consider those children to now be their family. It is what they must do. It is the right thing."

Daisy's heart swelled as she thought of the desperate straits that Maysa and the children lived in. She knew that in a camp like this, they were in desperate need of clean drinking water, as well as anything to burn so they could cook.

"Miss? Where do you come from?" Abia's curious eyes latched onto Daisy as she sat down next to her. Was she going to be the next generation of Yemeni women who would be eking out a living caring for other people's children?

"I come from America," Daisy smiled.

"Oooooh," Abia sighed, her eyes wide.

"Where do you come from, Abia?" Daisy asked.

Abia looked up at her mother.

"Sana'a," Maysa said wistfully. "That is where I met your father." She turned to Daisy. "I do not understand how I could help you."

"My job is to help women around the world, but first I need to understand what they need. I know that there are currently agencies working night and day to provide food, water, shelter, and medical care to everyone they can. But what is something else that can be done?"

Maysa kept her eyes down, not answering her question.

"Maysa, this is important. My job is to help women all over the world. During war and famine, women have different needs than men. Our troubles are different. Our sacrifices are often greater, but people don't notice. It is my job to notice. I have many people who work with me, and we find ways to help. But we can't help if people don't tell us what needs to be done."

"You can't help," Maysa whispered. "It is always the same."

"You're right, there is no way I will ever be able to help if I'm not told what the problem is, but if you tell me, then there is a possibility I can." Daisy prayed that her Arabic was good enough that Maysa was understanding her. "Please tell me a woman's problem."

Maysa looked up, her eyes determined.

"A family with a man is sometimes better."

Daisy waited for her to say more, but she didn't.

"How is it better?"

"The man can help to build a better home, sometimes with stones, so it will be warmer. He can sometimes find work or food while the woman cooks and cares for the children. Do you understand?"

Daisy nodded. "Go on."

"We need more aid than the households with a man, but that is not taken into consideration when aid is distributed."

What Maysa said made perfect sense, and Daisy didn't see that ever changing. The aid organizations were working hard to be scrupulously fair in their distribution of supplies. The only time a woman would get more is if she were pregnant or breastfeeding. Then she would almost need even more aid, because she wouldn't be able to cook for her family, or go out to the community well and get water for her family. The women were in a catch-22. Which was the whole reason W.A.N.T. had been started.

One-quarter of the families here in the internally displaced person camp were headed by women. Quick math told Daisy she was dealing with about two-hundred-and-fifty-thousand. The task seemed insurmountable. Even though W.A.N.T. was now bringing in hundreds of millions of dollars a year, there was no way they could cover feeding that number of people daily, and still continue their other endeavors.

"Maysa, this is exactly the kind of information I need. I'm going to be here for the next two weeks. I am going to have some of my teammates coming here too. Can I come back and ask you more questions?"

"Yes," Maysa smiled.

"Is it possible that you can bring other women to talk to us?"

The woman nodded.

"Thank you."

IT WAS the fourth time he'd left a voicemail, and three texts had gone unanswered. If he had the sense God gave a gnat, he'd give up.

"That's the third time you've looked at your phone in the last half-hour," his sister Maria teased him.

He looked up and realized that everyone around the dining room table was looking at him. Most of them had grins on their faces. *Assholes.* Except for his Mama—he could never say anything bad about her.

"*Mijo*, is something wrong?" his mother asked.

Leo sighed. "No, Mama."

"You haven't said a word all evening," she coaxed. "Tell us what's wrong."

He looked around the table at all the amused faces of his brothers and sisters and managed not to wince.

"That's not true, Mama. I told you that your dress looked gorgeous on you, and I've never seen you look more beautiful."

"Kiss ass," his brother Martin coughed under his breath. He was seated next to Leo.

Leo had to fight back a laugh.

"Yes, you did. You've always been so sweet."

"Mama's right," his oldest sister, Therese agreed. Butter wouldn't melt in her mouth. "And because you're so sweet, you're going to tell us what has you so preoccupied. Mama is bound to be worried. Is it a girl?"

The look he shot his sister promised retribution.

"Is it? Is it a girl?" his mother asked. It was her fondest wish that the last of her chicks would get married. That would be Leo.

He couldn't lie. "Yes, Mama, it's a girl. But, she's someone I met while overseas. So don't be thinking wedding bells. She's not local."

He watched as her mother's face fell, and felt like all kinds of a heel. "But she lives in the States, she just works a lot overseas."

"When can we meet her?" his mother pressed.

Ah fuck. I sure put my foot in it this time.

"That's the problem, Mama, she's not returning my messages."

Martin and Luis hooted with laughter.

"Our baby brother has finally met his match," Luis crowed.

"Leave your brother alone," their mother admonished. "It's okay, *Mijo*, she'll call you. Of course, she'll call you." Her faith in him was blinding.

He looked around the table. His sisters were all nodding, his brothers were all smirking. Yep, it was a typical dinner at the Perez family table.

———

"So, who is the girl?" Martin asked later when they were outside on the back porch watching the myriad nieces and nephews playing on the jungle gym that their parents had set up in the backyard.

"She's a bigwig at an international charity."

Martin took a sip of his beer.

"So you met her while you were working overseas? Did it have anything to do with the doctor who was rescued?"

Leo was done trying to figure out how Martin always put two and two together. Martin was a detective with the Virginia Beach Police Department. He'd been a police officer for over twenty years. As a child he could put a puzzle together faster than anybody he'd known, he was the kid who figured out the plot of the movie a third of the way in. So of course he could put together the fact that when Leo was 'out of town' and someone like Doctor Squires had been rescued, that he and his team would have something to do with it.

"You know I can't answer that," Leo said to his brother.

"Yeah, I know. But it's funny how the daughter of the good doctor manages a humongous international charity."

Leo glared at his brother.

"Just saying." He held up his hands.

Leo rolled his eyes. "Don't you have a case you should be working on?"

"Sure, it's called getting my brother married off."

"Aren't you supposed to be supplying Mom with great-grandchildren?"

"Bite your tongue, my daughters are still in college!"

Leo laughed and took a long sip of his Pacifico beer, then shouted at his nephew. "Derek, play nice with Lyndsey, or you have to come inside."

"Uncle," came the plaintive whine.

"If you're not careful, I'll also tell your grandmother you want to help with the dishes."

Martin and Leo chuckled as they watched Derek start to push Lyndsey on the swing.

"So what are you going to do about *the* Ms. Squires?" Martin asked.

"If she's not careful, I'm going to take a few days off and show up where she works. But first I need to make sure she's in-country."

"Why not just fly out to wherever the hell she is? Or are you afraid of going out of the United States?" Martin asked with a raised eyebrow.

Leo laughed. "Guess not. But first I want to figure out the lay of the land."

"So what's been stopping you?"

"We didn't part well."

"What did you do?" Martin asked.

"My job. But I felt like shit about it. I let her down."

"I don't know much, just read about the doc and his family. But it seems to me that anyone like this daughter of his would understand about your job and the constraints you have to live by. If she doesn't, then she's not the right one for you."

Leo didn't say anything, he just watched the kids rioting around the backyard. The sad part was, he really wanted her *to* understand. She was the first woman he'd ever imagined bringing home to this menagerie. What would she think about it?

"Leo?"

"Hmmm?"

"So are you going to hunt her down?"

Leo grinned. "I don't see as though I have any choice."

"Good man."

IT WAS THE BEGINNING OF HER THIRD WEEK IN YEMEN, AND she was beyond exhausted. They needed to come up with a new word. But looking at the women who had a houseful of children to care for, not enough food, and were still keeping on, Daisy knew she couldn't bitch. Hell, she at least had water and food!

She hiked up the toddler on her hip and made sure that he was sucking on the life-saving package of peanut butter nutrient as she tried to find what tent he'd wandered away from. Abia was holding on to her long shirt and once again jabbering away in Arabic.

"Sweetheart, are you sure you know where his mother is?" Daisy asked for the third time.

Again the girl nodded and pointed.

Daisy had to get back to the aid station. Three of her directors were coming in today from the states. She wanted to give them a tour and see what their thoughts were about what W.A.N.T. could get done for the displaced women here in this specific camp in Yemen. If they could set up something here that was effective, it could be a model that they could use for different camps across Yemen, then spread to different countries. But Daisy would need their brainpower.

"There!" Abia tugged hard at her shirt. For once the little boy seemed to be showing some interest in something other than Daisy's necklace.

How the little girl seemed to know everything that was going on in the camp was beyond Daisy, but over the last couple of weeks, she'd learned to roll with it.

"Lais," a woman in a worn blue skirt hollered out. The boy dropped his food and let go of Daisy's St. Christopher charm and yelled out for his mother. She mopped her eyes with the sleeve of her shirt as she ran toward them. All the way over to them, she thanked Daisy profusely for finding her son.

It was no wonder that someone would get lost in this camp that teemed with over a quarter-million people. Lais grabbed at his mother as Daisy picked up the little packet of food and wiped off the dirt. When she realized it was unsalvageable, she grabbed another one from her backpack and handed it to the mother who took it gratefully. They went off to their tent.

"Come, Abia, shouldn't you be learning your letters with your sister?" Daisy asked of the young girl.

She gave Daisy a sour look. "I like being with you."

"If you want to do great things one day, you must learn your letters. Let's go to your home, and you can practice. After you are done with your learning and your chores, you may ask your mother if you can spend some time with me tomorrow, how does that sound?"

"I want to spend time with you today," the little girl whined.

"I'm busy today. It will have to be tomorrow." Daisy

was firm. It was the only way with this strong-willed little girl.

"Okay. But I don't like it."

Daisy had to bite back a laugh. This kid was killing her.

"Duly noted."

She took her hand and they walked back to Maysa's tent. When Maysa saw her, she raised her eyebrows and shook her head. Daisy shrugged. The women were in perfect accord. There was no stopping the little girl, she was a firecracker. Daisy loved seeing that spurt of energy and defiance when the girl was undernourished and living with so many in their small little tent. She had such a will. This little girl could grow up to change the world.

When she got to the aid station, she was met by a shock. Besides her directors of development, operations, and public affairs, there was Rayi Abad.

And Leo Perez.

One she was happy to see, the other she was stunned to see. Daisy honestly thought Leo would have given up on her by now.

"Daisy, these gentlemen assured us you would want to have them tag along. Rayi said that he would be able to help provide some much-needed publicity for this project, and I couldn't agree more," Annie Cartwright smiled. She was fifty-two and an experienced Director of Development that Daisy had stolen from the Red Cross two years ago.

"Yes, Rayi is great. He helped me on a project in Afghanistan not so long ago. Has he told you his resume?" Daisy asked.

"Yes, he has. It's formidable."

"I approved Leo coming along," Doug Prentiss said.

"He said he would be available for the next two weeks to do some security evaluations. I couldn't be happier." Doug gave her a long, meaningful look. "For many reasons."

I'm going to kill Doug. I'm going to kill him in his sleep.

"Doug's a great guy, Daisy." Leo smiled easily. "We really hit it off."

"I'm sure you did," Daisy said through gritted teeth. She and Doug had worked together the longest. He was her mentor, but he lacked the leadership skills, nor did he want to run W.A.N.T., but he absolutely loved to stick his nose into Daisy's personal life. Not that she ever had one. That had never stopped Doug from trying to get her one. Now Leo showed up, and Doug looked as happy as a pig in mud.

"Daisy, I've got a few ideas about the project I want to run past you." Effie Long said as she handed her a list. "I've highlighted the most important points in pink. As the developmental director, I have to tell you, I don't think your vision is doable, but there are parts of it we could accomplish."

Doug and Annie laughed. Effie always had concerns about everything. That was her position, and she played it well.

"Okay, we'll go to the aid center and get you settled. Like usual, you'll have cots and on every fourth day you get to have a camp bath."

"Sounds about right," Effie sighed. "Okay, I have a set of notes for you to review. I didn't think we needed the reporter or the security analyst, but I bowed to Annie and Doug."

"I agree with Annie. Rayi will be a great addition to the team. But you might be right about Leo. We'll see if he really brings anything useful to the party." Daisy gave

Leo a laser-like glare. He gave her a heated smile in return. Once again she could hear Doug and Annie laughing.

Great. Just great.

———————

SHE LOOKED PISSED. Exhausted, but pissed. It was pretty damned funny. Leo worked hard to keep a straight face. He'd lucked out getting on the same bus as Daisy's executives to take to the internally displaced person camp here in Aden from the airport. After watching the interaction between Daisy and her personnel he could see that his take on the players had been pretty spot on. Effie, Doug, and Annie were all true believers in the cause. Annie and Doug would both take bullets for Daisy, but it was Doug who would kill Leo if he made one wrong move. On the bright side, he thought Daisy needed a personal life, and he didn't believe for an instant that Leo was here to provide security. He had totally caught on that Leo's reason for being here was personal, and he was happy about it.

"Leo, what a surprise to see you. I'm sorry if you didn't catch on to the message I was giving you."

"Daisy, I didn't get any message from you, so there was nothing to catch on to. Now that we're here together, hopefully, we can rectify that."

Dough laughed.

Effie looked confused.

Daisy glared at him. She was not happy. *Good, serves her right.*

"How do you two know each other?" Annie asked.

"We met in Afghanistan," Leo answered.

"I wondered," the reporter said. "I would like to ask you some questions."

Leo turned on him. "I have some questions of my own. Perhaps we can spend a little time alone later today," Leo all but growled. He was still pissed to find out that the reporter who had shown the video to Daisy was here in Yemen with her. He was not convinced this guy was on the side of the angels.

"Maybe you two can talk now," Daisy said sweetly. "I need to speak to my directors before we take a tour of the camp."

"After our talk, I think it is important that Leo be included on the tour," Doug piped up.

"Fine," was all Daisy said.

Leo smothered his grin.

"Where shall we meet you?"

"I'll show you where the aid station is. There is a small spot where you can onload your belongings. If you stay close, then we can find you. I could call you if you had a satellite phone."

"I do," Rayi said.

"Same," Leo agreed.

"Okay, then you can go further. But if you go too far, then we'll leave without you for the tour."

Again, he had to smother a grin. There was no give in the woman at the moment. Leo would have thought she was really pissed at him, but he knew better. She would have said unequivocally that he couldn't be part of the team, no matter what Doug said. She hadn't done that. So, she wasn't *that* mad at him. *Score one for Team Perez.* Still didn't explain why she'd ghosted him on all his texts and phone calls. Had she really believed he wouldn't contact her in the States? Why was she pushing him away after he'd kept his promise? But he'd wait to find out. It was good enough just being here and getting some face-time with the woman.

He watched as the four people walked away, then he turned to Rayi, who immediately started speaking to Leo in English.

"So you were on the rescue mission for Dr. Squires?" the reporter asked.

"No comment."

"But you're American special forces, right?"

"No comment."

"You and your Navy SEAL team were flown into Bagram Air Station five days before the rescue, then you were flown out ten hours after Dr. Squires was checked into the hospital at Bagram Air Base. I would say that you were part of the rescue. What do you have to say to that?"

"How do you know this?"

"There is very little that goes on in Afghanistan that I don't know about."

"I would say that you should focus on W.A.N.T., and what they are doing here. Otherwise, I might start asking you a lot of questions about why you would show a grieving daughter video of her father being beaten and tortured."

Rayi looked taken aback. "What are you talking about?"

"Why did you show her that? Why not just show her a picture of her father instead of the whole video? Are you a sadist, or what?"

"Mr. Perez, do you really think that woman would have been satisfied with just a picture? If you do, then you really don't know who you're dealing with."

"Tell me why in the hell you're here," Leo demanded, changing gears.

"Daisy Squires is of interest to many people. What she accomplishes will make a good article, and I intend to tell her story while she is here in Yemen."

"How did you get your hands on that video?"

Rayi laughed. "Really, Mr. Perez, your interrogation techniques leave something to be desired. I am not going to reveal my sources. I promised Daisy's stepfather that I would help her while she was in Afghanistan, and that's what I did."

"It sure seems like you have a source within the terrorist organization," Leo accused.

"Tell me something, did you not get your hands on the exact same video?" Rayi watched Leo closely. But Leo gave nothing away.

"Rayi. Leo. It's time for the tour," Daisy called out.

18

"You've got bruises under your eyes, and you've lost at least ten pounds in the three weeks since I saw you. Fuck yeah, I had Doug railroad you," Leo hissed under his breath so the others couldn't hear him.

They made their way up to the front of the line, and Leo stepped back so Daisy could check herself in. Leo had been impressed with Effie's efficiency. Not only had she arranged hotel rooms for the W.A.N.T. team, she'd gotten rooms for him and Rayi in this nice, downtown Aden hotel.

Leo laughed to himself. As much as Daisy bitched, he couldn't help but notice that she waited for him to finish checking in before she headed for the elevators.

"You waited," he smiled.

"I was waiting for the others," she said haughtily.

He took a moment to look around, "they've all gone upstairs."

She blushed. "Oh. I must be more tired than I realized."

He took the opportunity to take her backpack and duffel from her.

"I can carry that," she protested.

"So can I. This way we have a little bit of time to discuss why you've been ghosting all of my texts and calls for the last few weeks."

"That's easy. I was busy, didn't you notice?"

Leo rolled his eyes and took her elbow. "Come on, let's get you up to your room."

She yawned.

He needed to get her to her room immediately so she could sleep twelve hours through. Hell, maybe even twenty-four hours.

He ushered her to the elevator. He took note of the fact that two businessmen chose not to share the elevator with them. He was happy that Daisy didn't seem to notice. The woman needed a shower. When they got to her floor she was having trouble figuring out which way to go.

"Daisy, what's your room number?"

"Huh?"

"Give me your key."

She handed it to him.

"Come on, Honey, this way." He put his arm around her waist, to make sure she made it. As soon as he opened the door to her room, she gave a muffled sigh.

"Want shower. But need sleep." She looked at Leo, her eyes were filling with tears. "I'm so grungy." She yawned.

He wasn't so sure she could stay upright in the shower either.

"How about I stay here, to make sure you don't fall over in the shower?" He almost offered to shower with her, but that would be crossing a line.

She nodded. "Yes, please."

She swayed as she headed back toward the bathroom.

"Daisy, don't lock the door, in case I need to come in and help you."

"S'okay," she nodded. She left the door wide open, proving that she was at the end of her rope. Leo swung it almost closed, so he could hear her if she needed him. Then he went about the business of unpacking her clothes. Talk about grungy. He could see one section of clothes that she had rinsed out at one point and she probably planned to wear tomorrow, but they could use a good cleaning.

He called down to the front desk and asked if they could send somebody up to gather her garments for a laundry service. They promised to send someone right up. In the meantime, he pulled out one of his black T-shirts for her to wear. He snuck into the bathroom and pulled her dirty clothes off the floor and left his T-shirt on the sink.

The shower seemed to be reviving her, since she wasn't leaning against the wall of the shower.

Don't stare, don't stare, don't stare.

He left with the dirty clothes and added them to the pile. There was a knock on the door. He opened it to a woman who held out a laundry bag so Leo could put all of the clothes inside.

"These will be returned tomorrow," she promised in English.

"Thank you," he said in Dari. She gave him a shy surprised smile.

Leo closed the door, then heard the water shut off in the bathroom. He waited what seemed like forever for more movement. When he didn't hear the shower door open, he knocked.

"Daisy?"

"Yeah?" she said.

"You all right?"

Even from outside the bathroom he could hear her sigh. "Yeah. I think so."

God, she sounded so fragile.

"Honey, do you need help?"

"Yeah. I think I do."

Fuck.

He pushed open the door. She was still in the shower with her head leaning against the tiled wall. Because of her big personality, he often forgot just how small she was. He was in the bathroom like a shot, and had the shower door open with his arm around her before she had a chance to fall down.

She was shuddering.

"I'm fine, I can do this." Even her voice was trembling. She was totally lying.

He picked her up and took her into the bedroom and laid her down on the bed.

"I'm getting it wet."

"Just this side. Hold on, I'll get a towel."

He was back with all of the towels in the bathroom. She was curled up on her side. Now instead of just trembling, he could see goosebumps. "I'm cold."

The fact that she was cold in this hot room told him that she was past her last drop of endurance.

He pulled her up and gently wrapped a large bath towel around her as he pulled her onto his lap. He took another towel and started to squeeze the excess water out of her hair. He looked into her face and concern raced through him. He'd never seen her look so pale, not even when she'd been so distraught over her father. Then she smiled. Not the biggest or happiest smile, but it was something.

"Yes, Ms. Squires? What are you smiling about?"

"Are you destined to take care of me in hotel rooms?" she asked.

He laughed out loud. "Sure seems like it."

Her eyes opened and he saw a little bit of a twinkle in those beautiful gray eyes. "That was it," she slurred.

He could barely hear her. Then she yawned.

"What did you say, Honey?"

"That was it, I have no more witty banter," she sighed. "Sleep now." She cuddled up against him, like a kitten against a warm brick. He held her tighter and continued to dry her hair. When he heard the soft snuffles as sleep took her, his heart turned over. No wonder he'd tracked her down to the ends of the earth.

When her hair was mostly dry, he got up with her still in his arms, went around to the other side of the bed, and pulled down the covers. Carefully, he placed her into the bed and pulled up the covers. Her eyes drifted open.

"Don't leave."

"Honey, I've got to."

"Why?" She sounded so sad.

He had to leave; her defenses were down, and when she'd been thinking logically she'd decided not to see him. He needed to have her awake and conscious to make the decision for him to stay.

He picked up her hand and kissed her palm. Then he went over to her backpack and found her satellite phone. He brought it back to her. "If you need me, call me. Night or day, I'll be here."

"Promise?"

"I promise."

"WHAT'S YOUR STORY?" Doug asked.

Leo had to laugh at the older man who had basically barged into his room with a fifth of single malt scotch.

"An Englishman bearing gifts. Aren't I supposed to be suspicious?" Leo asked as he pulled two glasses from the bathroom.

"No, that's Greeks bearing gifts. You're safe with me, except I plan to get you drunk and figure out your intentions regarding our esteemed leader."

"Well, let's get that bottle open, shall we?" Leo put the glasses down on the nightstand between the two standard beds and Doug poured.

"How long have you been working with Daisy?" Leo asked.

"Since she started working for W.A.N.T. as an intern. That would be eight years ago. She was a dynamo then, and she's only gotten stronger as the years have gone on. I started working as her subordinate four years ago when she took over. She took it internationally and made us into one of the big boys. She's a good boss."

"What was she like back then, besides being a dynamo?" Leo asked as he took a sip of the smooth liquor.

"She was young, obviously. Led with her heart, never wanted to hurt anyone's feelings. It took her a couple of years to build up a callous so she could do what needed to be done. This is not a job for the faint of heart."

"She became hard?"

"Not hard exactly, but she could make the hard decisions. We can't save everybody, but what is the best use of our funds and resources? She can make that determination now. What I don't understand is why she was working herself into a frazzle at this camp. She knows better than that."

Leo knew. It was because of her revelation with her father. He'd seen how it made her question herself, and this was the result. He hated this.

"What? What do you know?"

"Huh?"

"Don't play dumb with me, Son. I've dealt with the dumbest sons of bitches on God's green earth. You're not in their league. So do you know what's wrong with Daisy? Is it because of you that she's acting so out of character?"

Leo rested his elbows on his knees. "No, sir, it's not. It's her father."

"Alistair?"

"Nope, the other one."

"Shit, I should have bloody figured. I thought everything went okay when he got rescued. Normally she doesn't have much to say about him. As long as he got out alive, I figured it wouldn't much touch her."

Leo looked up at the man from under his brows.

"You don't want to tell me? Or can't tell me?"

Leo shrugged.

"Hmmm. I tagged you as military right off. Might have had a little something with the duffel bag," Doug grinned. "But the habit you have of not saying much of anything tells me you've been around the block a time or two."

Leo took another sip of his scotch.

"I'll just ask you outright. Are you good for her?"

"I really think I am, Doug. But that's got to be for her to decide, now doesn't it?"

"Yep, I like you." Doug clinked his glass against Leo's.

"Ouch," she mumbled. What in the hell was digging into her shoulder?

Daisy sat up and realized it was her satellite phone. She'd been sleeping on it. How had that happened?

God, she was hot.

She pushed off the covers and realized she was stark naked. This was so not how she normally slept. She looked around the room and it took her more than a minute to remember what happened. She looked down at the end of the bed and saw a black T-shirt waiting for her. She knew immediately it was Leo's.

Looking over at her duffel and backpack, she could see how empty they were. He must have sent out her laundry to guest services. She turned on her satellite phone. What time was it? For that matter, what day was it?

Getting out of bed, she slipped on the shirt and then grabbed her vanity case out of her bag and took it into the bathroom. After she was done in there and her teeth were actually brushed she felt halfway human. It was ten in the morning. There were still bruises underneath her eyes, but now she didn't look like a zombie, so score one for sleep.

She grabbed one of the bottles of water that the hotel had provided then sat back down on the bed and started to scroll through her messages. Her team had handled almost everything that she had been contacted about. She loved these people. She had almost finished her bottle when her phone rang. It was Leo.

"Hello."

"You sound much better. You're not even slurring your words." She could hear the smile in his voice.

"I feel much better." She put down the bottle, then

switched ears with the phone. "I really appreciate your help yesterday."

"It wasn't any problem. I was just glad to help."

Daisy felt her cheeks heat. "You mean you would have done that for anyone?"

"I probably wouldn't have cuddled one of my teammates in my lap, no." Leo chuckled.

If she blushed anymore, she'd suffer from heatstroke.

"You still there?" he asked.

"Yeah."

"You're blushing, aren't you?"

"Yeah."

"You know, for someone who runs an international charity, you sure do like one-syllable answers."

This time it was her turn to laugh.

"I'd really like to see you today, Daisy."

"I have to go back to the camp."

"The others, including Rayi, have already left."

"They *what*?"

"You snooze, you lose. Everybody figured you could use the extra sleep."

"But I need to show them around."

"Annie already talked to the head man at the Red Cross and arranged for a tour. They're set for today. Doug said to tell you that tomorrow you can set up a tour with the ladies you want your team to meet."

"Goddammit, Leo. I don't like this. I wanted to go."

"Daisy, you have to admit you're burnt out. According to Doug, he's never seen you like this, not even when you first started. You know you need to cut yourself some slack."

Her gut reaction was to fight back and tell him he was wrong, but she took a moment to really think. "I'm not sure that I can," she whispered. "I've gotten so many things wrong. What if how I've been running things has been wrong? Maybe I'm too hands-off? I sit in my office, moving chess pieces around on the board, playing God. How can I possibly do that without walking in their shoes?"

"I'm coming upstairs."

"What are you talking about? I'm fine, Leo."

"You better damn well open the door when I knock."

"Leo, I don't..." She was talking to thin air.

19

THE DOOR OPENED BEFORE HE EVEN KNOCKED ON IT.

He stared down at her shining, beautiful face and glared. "Tell me you looked through the peephole."

"I just wanted to prove you didn't even have to knock."

"Daisy," he growled.

She held up her hands. "I looked, I looked." Her eyes were twinkling. Well, that was better. He'd been worried that she'd been spiraling. Oh, who the hell was he kidding? He was still worrying.

"Leo, don't look at me like that, I'm going to be just fine. And why is it that you always have to find me in hotel rooms when I'm falling apart?" She damn near flounced to the bed and sat down. He noticed that her linen pants and white shirt were clean. The laundry service had really come through.

"You never fall apart. You're one of the strongest people I've ever met."

"Bullshit. You're a SEAL, you hang around with SEALs. I cried all over you because of fucking daddy issues. Don't tell me I'm strong." She shot back up off the bed and started to rip off the blankets and tugging up the sheets.

"What are you doing?"

"What does it look like? I'm making the bed. I always make the bed. I just hadn't gotten around to it yet."

Leo went to the other side and started pulling up the sheet.

"Stop it. I can do it myself."

Leo ignored her and continued to help.

"You're not going to listen to me, are you?" she asked.

"I will when you tell me something worthwhile."

"What, you think the whining I was just doing over the phone was worthwhile? Me being upset because I can't figure if I should or shouldn't be at the camp? Whether I should or shouldn't be working in the States? Sure, Leo, who the hell wants to hear that load of crap?"

She grabbed the comforter off the floor and swung it over the bed. Leo grabbed his side and then let it waft over the bed.

"I *want* to hear that crap. Haven't you figured it out yet that I want to spend time with you and hear all about you, the insignificant minutia, the things that trouble you, the heart-wrenching and the funny. I want to hear it all."

Her eyes went wide. "Are you high? We've known each other for three days," she scoffed.

Leo could have taken it as a gut punch, but he had three older sisters and two teenage nieces. He could see the vulnerability that Daisy was working so hard to hide. And he could hardly blame her for still being angry that he'd ghosted on her when she needed him the most. *That's the story of her life.* And it was up to him to convince her that he was the next chapter.

"We'll take this a step at a time, okay?"

Her eyes narrowed. "What does that mean?"

"Finish telling me what you started on the phone before I came up here."

"No. I was just being a whiny baby."

Leo went over to the window, sat down on the sill, and folded his arms. He waited.

"You think that tactic is going to work on me?" she asked.

He didn't say anything, just raised an eyebrow.

"Seriously Leo, I'm sick of hearing all the crap swirling around in my brain, why would *you* want to hear it?"

Once again she sat down on the bed. "I mean seriously. Where is my time better spent? At the home office, where I can really help bring in the money and coordinate the resources, or figuring out where W.A.N.T. is truly needed? And if it is on the ground, how can I do that without spending time with them? Did you see the girl? Abia? My God, Leo, she is so bright, she has so much potential, but the conditions she's living in are horrific, and when you add on the fact that she's living in a household run by a woman, she doesn't stand a chance. What can I do?"

In four long strides, Leo was in front of her, then he knelt down. He put his hands on her knees. "Honey, you're so tired you can't see the forest for the trees. You're not the same person I met three weeks ago. I've seen this happen so many times before. Have you ever been in-country like this when you were trying to help?"

"Sure, all the time. There was Haiti, the Philippines, Guatemala, and the Sudan."

"When was that?" His thumbs rubbed circles on her knees.

"The last time was probably five years ago. Since then

I've been more administrative."

"Bullshit—you're not administrative, you're running the whole damn thing. Now, what did you do when you were in the field?"

"I helped where I could, and I submitted reports to recommend where funds could be best spent."

"Could you have made the decisions of where to spend the money back then?"

She shuddered. "God, no. I would have wanted to spend all the money, wherever I was at the moment."

He nodded. "Exactly. That's what's going on right now. That's why you're spiraling."

For long moments she looked down at his hands. Finally, she looked up, her eyes fierce. "What is my fucking problem? How could I have not seen that?"

"Probably because you've not had food or sleep, would be my guess," Leo gave a slight chuckle.

"How dumb could I be?"

"Don't call my girlfriend dumb."

Daisy threw back her head and laughed. "I heard that. Thought you could sneak that by me, did you?"

"Like I said, you're in a vulnerable state, you can't see the forest for the trees. Seemed like a good time to stake my claim. Plus..." His voice lowered.

His eyes heated.

She shivered. "Plus what?"

"You're sitting on a bed. In a hotel room, and..." His voice was a whisper.

He could see her eyes dilate. "And what?"

"Nobody is expecting us to be anywhere, and I'm here in front of you. Where I want to be. On my knees."

"Bloody hell," she moaned.

She grabbed his hair and angled her head. Her

pillowy soft lips collided with his and his brain went haywire. Her tongue parted his lips and Leo relished her aggression. He wrapped his arms around her waist and stood up, taking her with him. He curved one arm under her ass and coaxed her legs around his waist, turning so that he sat on the bed. She straddled him. It was perfect.

He stroked his hands down her glossy brown hair, luxuriating in the satin feel. Then his hand drifted along her neck, slowly tracing down her soft skin toward the first tantalizing button of her linen blouse. One button undone. Two buttons undone. Then the third. And the fourth. All by touch as he continued to let her take him to dizzying heights with her kiss.

Leo had never let a woman take the lead like this. Daisy's small hand gripped the nape of his neck, pulling him closer. He smiled against her lips when he heard a feminine growl as she clutched him even tighter. It was as if she wanted one damn thing at this moment that she could control, and if he was it, he was happy to oblige. But when she started to grind the molten heat between her thighs against his erection, it took everything in him to continue to let her command the situation.

"Daisy," he groaned. "I didn't bring condoms with me. They're in my room."

"Bad Boy Scout," she glowered. "I'm on birth control. Are you good with that?"

His dick leapt for joy. "God yes. Are you?"

"Oh yes," she said before she went in for another soul-shattering kiss.

He pulled her shirt open and flicked open the front clasp of her white cotton bra. Touching her breasts was like touching warm silk. He clasped the slight weight in his hand, relishing how she fit perfectly against his palm, her tight nipple throbbing against his hand, begging for a deeper touch. How could he deny her body anything? He circled her areola with his thumb, gratified at her moan of pleasure.

"More," she gritted out.

He continued with the teasing touch, knowing what she wanted, but wanting her to ask. That had been such a fun game three weeks ago. Round and round, his thumb revolved around the soft skin, waiting...

He jerked when she bit his bottom lip, then he laughed.

"Harder," she growled. "You know what I want. Harder."

Once again he was happy to oblige. He dipped his head and sucked her nipple into his mouth, twirling his tongue around the tender nub. She gripped his head, trying to pull him closer, but she was no match for his strength. Her nails bit into his scalp, signaling her desire. Delicately, he bit her nipple and she groaned her satisfaction.

"Yesss. Oh, Leo. Yesss."

He massaged her other breast, pinching and torturing the nub as she pushed her chest closer to him. She was glorious. She was going to kill him.

It was long minutes of pleasure for both of them before she shoved him away. "I want more. Clothes off now." Her eyes glittered with desire and determination.

He lifted off the bed with her in his arms, then let her slide slowly to the floor, letting her sensuous body torture his. She reached for his belt and fumbled. Then she stopped and looked up at him.

"Fuck it. It's too slow that way. Strip," she commanded.

He laughed again. Laughter and loving, could it get

any better?

"Aye, aye."

He pulled his T-shirt over his head and then looked at her watching him. "No fair," he said. "You're not stripping, you're just watching."

"No woman with a pulse would blame me." Her tongue ran across her bottom lip.

"You better strip, Woman, otherwise I'm tearing off those clothes, got it?"

She gulped. "You wouldn't... Would you?"

"Not only that, I'd use the strips to tie you to the bed."

Her eyes widened. He could tell she was intrigued. They didn't have time—maybe round two. "Daisy, strip," he ordered as he sat down on the bed to unlace his boots.

This time he got to watch.

She pulled off her shirt and bra, and he damn near fucked up the knot on his bootlace.

Concentrate!

He looked down and got his boots and socks off in record time.

"Hurry," she said as she skimmed out of her pants.

He got up and unbuckled his belt and pulled down his pants.

"No underwear?"

He shrugged. "It's hot in Yemen." He looked at her in her little white lace panties. He picked her up and positioned her on the bed, then slowly, ever so slowly, slid her panties down her shapely legs.

She sucked in a deep breath, then sighed. He looked up into her eyes; she was his every dream.

"Here. Come here." She lifted her arms toward him. Leo slid up her body so they could be chest to breast, heart to heart.

"You feel so good. I feel so safe when I'm in your arms," she breathed into his neck.

Had any woman ever made him feel so good?

This time he started the kiss. A tender kiss, one that let her know how he felt—the care, the longing, the love. She parted her legs, her foot caressing the back of his calf. He felt the warm, wet welcome of her against his cock, but it wasn't enough. He had to be sure.

Sliding a hand down past her taut stomach, he parted her soft folds and lightly touched her delicate bundle of nerves. She jerked hard against his fingers.

"No, don't do that," she begged. "I'm too close. Together. I want us to fly together."

Her hand smoothed down his erection and guided him towards her entrance, and he was lost. He pushed home in one long glide, relishing her tight depths.

"God, Daisy, you're killing me."

She gasped. "My line. That's my line."

Her legs wrapped around him and she arched upward, taking more and more of him. She was a goddess as she reveled in the sensuality of their union. He breathed in the vanilla and orange blossom scent of her as she shared her pleasure, which reverberated back on him. Thrust after thrust in her snug, honeyed depths, robbing him of breath, he was just intent on making sure that she reached her pinnacle before he did.

Her nails scored his back, as she lunged upwards.

"Leo," she cried out, then her teeth gripped his shoulder as she shuddered beneath him, sparking his release into oblivion. His last thought was to wonder how was it possible that he felt surrounded and cared for, as if she had taken him to a place where their souls communicated as one.

20

"I NEED TO GET VIDEO OF ABIA," EFFIE SAID TO DAISY.

"Why?"

They were walking around the camp. Doug and Annie were back at the hotel trying to put together a proposal on how they might be able to funnel some monies toward this project. Effie came along with Leo, Rayi, and Daisy in her function as the Director of Public Affairs. She was outstanding in her job, and it was through her strategic thinking and her ability to tug at donors' heartstrings that Daisy could get so many donations.

"That smile. That enthusiasm. And I hate to say it, but when people realize she's five years old, that is going to kill them. They'll be opening up their wallets. I can't believe how emaciated all of the kids are around here."

Daisy stopped walking, her stomach churning at the thought of using Abia's underdeveloped body as a selling point.

"Hun, are you all right?" Effie asked.

Daisy just shook her head, trying to clear it. "I'm fine."

"You don't look like it." Effie dug in her oversized purse. "Here, have some water."

Daisy took it and drank a third of the bottle. It did help a little bit. She needed to be more careful. "Effie, I'm not sure I want to use Abia in that way."

"Hun, it will really help with the campaign. This is not going to be an easy sell, with everything else we have going on. I think we're going to need a lot of photos. Some drone footage so they can see the size of the camp, and some video of Abia and have her introduce her family. Trust me, this will work."

"We'll see."

Effie sighed.

Meanwhile, Rayi was taking notes of the conversation, which concerned Daisy. Leo was busy watching everybody and everything as if there were a bogeyman around every corner. Daisy really wished Annie and Doug were here.

"Miss!" Abia came running up to her. "Miss! Where were you yesterday? Mama said you might have gone home. Back to that place called America. Did you go home and come back?" the little girl asked.

"I told you," Effie whispered.

Daisy crouched down and smiled. Abia lifted her arms to be picked up.

Leo crouched down beside Daisy. "Would you like to ride on my shoulders? Then you would be up really high."

"Are you really big?" Abia asked.

Leo stood up to his full height. Abia clapped. "You are! Miss, can I ride his shoulders? Please." Daisy knew what Leo was doing; he was trying to make it so that Daisy didn't push herself. But since the little girl was so excited, she couldn't be *too* mad.

Leo grinned at Daisy, knowing he had won.

"You're a manipulator, you know that, don't you?" she whispered to him.

"I use my powers for good. You should know that," he purred. Daisy blushed. Yes, his powers definitely were good. Hell, they'd spent hour after decadent hour in bed, only getting up to go to dinner.

"Up!" Abia giggled. Her enthusiasm was contagious, causing all of the adults to smile. Leo carefully lifted her up onto his shoulders.

He showed her where to place her hands so she wouldn't fall down. He held her legs securely. They walked to her mother's tent. When Maysa let them in, she was all-smiles. Daisy took her time introducing everybody. She had prepped Maysa that she would be bringing visitors, and the woman was ready. She had a little plate of food waiting for them. Daisy felt like a heel taking any kind of food from the little family, but she knew to decline would be a grave insult.

"Thank you," she said in Arabic. "I am honored."

All four of them sat down in the tent and tasted the little stuffed bread that she had prepared. She had carefully cut the bread into four pieces for them. Maysa meanwhile took another piece of *malawah* and cut it into nine pieces for all of the children in the room who were wide-eyed at the treat. She couldn't help but notice that Maysa did not serve any to herself.

Leo looked around the little tent and smiled. He had put Abia on the ground. "Ma'am, would you allow me to tighten some of the sides so they don't wave as much?"

"I don't have tools or the proper stakes to push into the ground. But thank you for your concern," she gave a wistful smile.

Leo took off his backpack and pulled out stakes and a hammer. "If you would allow me?" His Arabic was very good.

Daisy could see the woman tearing up. Meanwhile, Daisy grabbed her backpack and took out another gallon of water and more of the peanut butter packs. Effie took her backpack off and took out some flour, rice, beans, and butter. Maysa turned away quickly to put away the supplies, but Daisy knew it was so nobody would see her crying.

When Maysa had gotten herself together, Effie and Daisy asked Maysa if they could discuss some ideas they had.

"Of course," Maysa said.

"It is important that people understand what you are going through," Effie explained kindly and Daisy translated. "My job is to get your story out to the world."

Maysa looked confused.

"Our organization can't help people without donations from businesses and individuals. We get those donations when we explain or show people just how badly someone like you or your children need them. Making a video of you helps to do that."

Maysa nodded. More people in the camp had phones than Daisy had expected. As people lined up for water, others would line up to use the generators to charge their cell phones. So Maysa might not get the concept of people across the world donating money because of what she would say on a video, but she certainly understood the idea of making a video.

Out of the corner of her eye, Daisy could see Leo making the tent sturdier. Four of the boys who lived with Maysa were watching him, fascinated. He was something else; who else would have thought to do this? And how in the hell had he found the hammer and stakes?

"Tell her, Daisy," Effie said.

"What? Oh yeah." Thank God she could multi-task. "Besides being in your tent, it would be wonderful if you could show us how you have used the aid center that the Red Cross has set up as well. Would that be possible? If you could take one of your children with you, that would be helpful."

"Did you say Abia?" Effie asked. "I didn't hear her name mentioned."

Daisy sighed. "My friend thinks that having Abia would be good, because of her smile."

At that, Maysa smiled too. "She is the song of my heart. But sometimes she can be full of mischief, that one."

Daisy laughed. She could see it. "We could come back tomorrow. Would that work?"

Maysa nodded.

"SO TELL me a little bit about your article," Leo asked Rayi.

"Yes, I'm interested as well," Doug said.

Leo had called Doug when they were in the car back from the camp. He knew he needed someone official from W.A.N.T. to back him while questioning Rayi, and Daisy wasn't objective enough. That's why Doug was lying in wait for Rayi and Leo when they came in through the lobby and had pulled them away from Effie and Daisy.

"What do you want to know?" Rayi asked pleasantly. "Shall we sit down?" He indicated some seats in the lobby.

"Let's," Leo said with a smile.

"I want to know what kind of bullshit article you're writing that people in Afghanistan would be interested in knowing about W.A.N.T.," Doug said.

"You underestimate the people of my country," Rayi said. "Also, you underestimate me. My articles are often picked up internationally, and I feel comfortable that this one will be as well."

"When Daisy gave you such close access did she put up any parameters? Did she say that Effie would have to review the article?" Doug asked.

Rayi's smile got big. "No, she did not."

"Fuck," Leo growled. "What the hell was she thinking? Scratch that. She hasn't been thinking, she's too tired."

"And she was too upset about her father," Rayi nodded. "This is true."

"And you're taking advantage of her?" Doug stood up and yelled down at Rayi. "What kind of man are you?"

Rayi didn't seem perturbed in the slightest. Leo started thinking of all the ways he would convince Rayi that he was not going to print this story.

"I did not say that I wasn't going to run the story past your public affairs department, I just said that Ms. Squires didn't request that of me. I am very aware of her vulnerable state of mind right now. I also know that is not normally her, and I don't intend to write her in that light. It would be a disservice to her and my readers."

Leo felt something ease off his chest. Maybe this Rayi guy wasn't all that bad.

"I don't want Effie to read it, I want to read it too," Doug said, still standing over Rayi.

"That is fine with me. Now, are we finished here?"

Leo and Doug both nodded.

---

*L*EO.

He's coming to my room tonight, right?

She swiped the razor against her right leg trying not to cut herself. That's what she needed—to be a bloody mess as she tried to seduce the man again. For God's sake, she'd attacked him last night.

Okay, only one nick, now for the other leg. Maybe her hand would be less shaky.

Don't think of Leo. Don't think of Leo.

God, his chest. His lips. His eyes.

It was his eyes that did it for her. He spoke with his eyes, and he seemed to be saying a lot of things. Things that she couldn't bring herself to believe. He couldn't be emotionally into her. She'd dated sometimes. There'd been that man—well, boy really—in Guatemala where they were both working on an assignment. He hadn't really cared. The only thing she allowed herself to care about was W.A.N.T. and family. *Not* her father. Because people let you down.

But Leo, he seemed to care, but she was just projecting her feelings onto him, wasn't she?

Ah fuck, I have feelings!

"Ouch!"

She looked down at the blood streaming down her leg. She felt frustrated tears welling up.

No feelings. No feelings. No feelings.

Feelings got you hurt. Expectations got you hurt. People always left you when you needed them the most.

So I'm stupid to expect Leo to come to my room tonight. He's seen who I am and changed his mind.

"And I shouldn't be shaving my legs!"

She looked down at her half-shaved leg. Well, she couldn't leave it like that, for God's sake. She finished up and then got out of the shower. She slathered some ointment on the cuts and it stopped the bleeding.

I'm going to read a book. I like books.

She put on a denim skirt and a yellow scoop neck T-shirt, then sat down on the bed and picked up her e-reader. She wasn't going to call him. He could call. He was good at calling. *I'm not projecting feelings, and I didn't see feelings in his eyes. There are no feelings. No such thing as feelings.*

She went through her list of books, looking for one that she could cry to, and found *To Kill a Mockingbird.*

21

IF HE SPENT ONE MORE SECOND IN HIS HEAD WONDERING why she hadn't called, he'd call Cullen for dating advice. Yep, that would be the kind of punishment he'd deserve for being so goddamned wishy-washy. But seriously, he'd followed her halfway around the world, followed her around the camp, come to her hotel door yesterday, and they'd made love all day and night. Not once had she made one call or come his way. Was he kidding himself?

"Fuck this noise. I'm not going to call Cullen. I'm taking a page out of Nic's playbook. He's all about assuming the win. God, twenty-four is so damn young. But I'm assuming the win."

He looked at his bare feet, then looked at his boots.

Fuck it. Assume the win. Taking off my boots just takes more time.

He left his room and ignored the couple who stared at his feet the entire time he was in the elevator.

He knocked on her door. It seemed like forever until she opened it.

"Please, for the love of God, say you used the peephole before you opened up the door wearing just a T-shirt."

"Of course I did. Where are your shoes?"

He squinted down at her. "Hey, wait a minute, that's my T-shirt."

"Possession is ninth-tenths of the law."

"Are you going to let me in? Or are we going to talk in the hallway?"

She backed up and he walked in. The bed wasn't made. As a matter of fact, she'd been in it, and he could see she had been reading on her e-reader.

"What are you reading?"

"I'm pretending I'm back in high school and reading *To Kill a Mockingbird*," she said.

"Harper Lee, damn good author. That book makes me tear up every time I read it."

"You re-read books?"

"My favorites, yes. I usually take a book with me each mission. Last time it was one of Mark Twain's."

"Reading gets me through the tough times," Daisy admitted to him.

Leo reached out, then drew back his hand. "This has been some of the toughest for you, hasn't it?"

"Full disclosure?" she asked quietly.

He nodded.

"Absolutely some of the toughest. But some of the best too. But I just don't believe in good like this. You know?"

Leo frowned and this time he did touch her cheek. "No. Explain it to me." He guided her to the bed, wishing there was a damned chair or something in the room. But nope, just the bed. He sat down beside her.

She nuzzled her cheek into the palm of his hand. "This isn't real."

"Yesterday afternoon and last night sure as hell felt real to me. Hell, even this morning when you woke up in my arms felt pretty damn real to me."

"Was it? Or is it just when we're in desperate times? How do I know this is real?"

Leo dropped his forehead so that it rested lightly on hers. "Is that how it feels to you? That our only connection is when emotions are high because of outside events, and it has nothing to do with you and me?" *I sure as hell hope not.*

He watched as Daisy processed his question. Her brain was such a turn-on, even when it went a little sideways, like now. He'd bet his bottom dollar that she didn't have much relationship experience to draw on, so this was tough for her.

"Let me ask this question another way; could you picture yourself having been comforted by someone else that day in Afghanistan? Ending up in another man's arms? Kissing another man? Taking another man into your body that afternoon?"

"God no," she gasped.

"Well then?"

Daisy cupped his cheeks and tried to kiss him.

"No, none of that. We did that yesterday and you ended up confused. We're getting this straightened out right now."

"But it was so good," she murmured.

"Absolutely it was. But I want to know that this has legs. Are you going to go sideways again and think this is only for hotel rooms in foreign countries? Because if you are, I'm opting out."

Shit, did I just say that?

She pulled back and looked at him. "Leo, I'm not using

you for a booty call. I heard you when you were 'teasing, not teasing' yesterday. You said girlfriend, right?"

He nodded.

"I'm not good at relationships, though. I work all the time, and I don't have balance or anything normal. Somebody thought I should have a cat once, and Effie thought we should start with a plant. It ended up dying."

He touched her hair. "It was from over-watering, right?"

It was her turn to nod.

"See, you don't neglect things, you just haven't figured out how to handle some aspects of life. Number one rule, respond to my damned texts."

She puffed out a laugh.

"Do you know what the number two rule is?"

"Answer your calls?"

"The girl gets an 'A'. Now tell me why you didn't."

"It's complicated."

"I have three sisters, of course it's complicated."

"I was kind of scared. You know, about it being too good and not real. I was afraid if I picked up you wouldn't be as good as I remembered, and then the good memory would go away. And Leo?" She grabbed his face again like she really wanted him to listen. "That was the best memory ever. I couldn't afford for it to go away."

If he'd been standing his knees would have gone weak. Her answer couldn't have been more perfect.

"And now?"

"I'm still scared," she breathed out. "Scared you'll still change your mind and leave for good."

He pulled her into his arms and she gave a small moan of pleasure.

"I'm here, I'm not going anywhere, and this will last," he whispered into her ear.

He felt her shaking her head.

"Okay, I'm here and we're going to make beautiful memories, moment, by moment, by moment, by moment. How about that?"

She nuzzled his neck.

"Yes, please. That I can believe in."

AT THE CAMP the next day, Daisy was trying to keep Maysa calm. She couldn't blame her for being nervous. Effie had outdone herself. Somehow, she had managed to scrounge up two cameramen with actual shoulder-mounted camcorders, with lights. She'd also found someone who could operate a drone to take aerial footage of the camp. The children were fascinated, but Maysa was nervous as hell.

"How did she find these people?" Leo asked Daisy.

"She's magic. Just like you found the hammer and the stakes."

"That was small potatoes. This is amazing." Leo took Daisy's empty water bottle and replaced it with a full one.

"Maysa, Effie has hired these gentlemen to help you tell your story. Their cameras are just like what is on a phone, only bigger."

Maysa shook her head in disbelief.

"Effie, can you get them to show her?"

"It's better if you do, Daisy. They're here because of you."

"What do you mean, me?"

"I used your name. They heard that you head W.A.N.T.

and that you are trying to get money for women in the camps. They wanted to help."

"But I don't understand, how did they hear about me?"

Effie turned to the first cameraman who was closest to them. It was clear he was trying to keep track of their conversation. "Daisy, this is Tahir."

"Hello, ma'am," he said in heavily accented English. "The other ma'am is correct. You are known."

"Talk to him in Arabic," Effie suggested. "He'll be able to explain better how he knows about you."

"It is an honor to meet you, Tahir," Daisy said. "How do you know of me?"

He smiled broadly. "My wife's second cousin spoke of you. Her friend is in the camp. You've spoken to her. You are trying to make her life better. You run a charity to get them help, so I want to help." He slapped his chest.

"As do I," the second cameraman piped up.

Daisy was stunned that word had gotten out about what she was doing.

"Miss!"

Everyone turned to see Abia running up toward Daisy with her arms up. Before Leo could intercept, Daisy was picking up the little girl.

"I missed you," Abia said as she smiled brightly.

"I missed you too," Daisy grinned.

"Who are they?" she pointed to the cameramen.

Tahir explained they were going to take pictures. Then, God bless him, he took a quick video of Effie and then replayed it for Maysa and Abia to see. Watching, Maysa nodded her head.

"Can we go over to your tent and take some video of you, your children, nieces and nephews? Then I'd like to ask you some questions. Would that be okay?"

Maysa nodded.

I sure hope she starts talking when we get to her tent.

Daisy was impressed when she noticed that both men were filming all the way down the long rows of tents as they made their way to Maysa's tent. It took them almost fifteen minutes to get there. As they walked along many people watched, some actually followed. But again, so many people were hot, tired, and hungry, they just didn't have the energy to give a damn.

Daisy took note of the men she now saw walking down the rows and nodded at Leo. When Maysa started feeling comfortable answering Effie's questions with Tahir acting as translator, Daisy fell back to talk to Leo privately.

"Who are they?" she asked him.

"Who's who?"

"Don't play innocent. Who are the men who are nodding to you?"

"I told you I was here to help with security. I got access to the camp by talking to the Red Cross about volunteering my services to consult on camp security. They were all over it. The UN Peacekeepers are sparse on the ground."

It was true.

"Who are these men?"

"They've been vetted. They all worked in law enforcement or the military before ending up here. They all volunteered, but before I tapped them, I found their records. They all made the cut."

"Effie isn't the only one working miracles today."

"I wish. I still can't get the Peacekeepers to let me make recommendations for the camp entrance, the food distribution site, or the aid station. They're driving me up the wall." Leo ran his hand through his hair.

"You'll convince them, I have faith."

"I only have another four days."

Shit, where has the time gone?

"How about you? What are your plans after you have the press release in the can?"

Abia finally had enough. She pulled at Daisy's necklace and patted her cheek. "Me," she said in Arabic. "Talk to me."

Leo chuckled.

"Okay, Darling. What do you want to talk about?"

"Can they take my picture?" She pointed to Tahir.

"I think that can be arranged. Let's get to your home first, okay?"

The little girl's eyes got wide with enthusiasm. Daisy could see just what a few weeks of extra food had done for her. The difference was amazing. But she still looked like she was no more than three years old, instead of five.

"Will they talk to my brothers and sisters? We can show them our drawings."

"That would be great. What did you draw?" Leo asked.

"I drew a cat. My brother drew an airplane. My other brother drew a soldier."

"We would love to see them. Maybe you could draw a flower." Daisy suggested. Abia looked at her funny.

"What are you trying to say," Leo asked.

"Flower," she said in English.

"You said 'fast'."

"No wonder she's looking at me weird. You translate."

Leo asked the girl if she could draw a flower for Daisy. He explained that Daisy's name meant flower. Abia clapped and said she would as soon as she got home. Maysa had done an incredible job of making her youngest child feel good about where she was living. Daisy knew it was tougher for the older children who remembered their real home before they had been displaced.

Abia scrambled down as soon as they arrived at their tent, and she found her coveted small notepad. Almost every page was covered with her little drawings.

"Come look," she Abia to Daisy and Leo. They walked around where Effie was having the cameramen set up. When the young girl showed her artwork, the other children began to bring out their notepads and show their artwork as well. She knew damn well that Effie was having them videotape this entire episode. She hated it, but she understood.

"Daisy, why don't you come here and interview Maysa," Effie called out. "Then we can tour the central areas."

Daisy looked up at Leo who gave her a head tilt. She smiled gratefully, knowing he'd continue with the kids.

It took about an hour with Maysa. She ended up speaking eloquently about the plight of the women who acted as heads of households here in the camp, and why they were especially disadvantaged. They would be a perfect demographic for W.A.N.T.'s donors.

"Okay, now to the central area," Effie said with a smile. "Thank you so much for your time, Mrs. Saleh. You have been a tremendous help." When Daisy translated the words, Maysa smiled shyly.

When everybody started to leave the tent, Abia begged her mother to let her go as well.

"No, you'll be in the way," Maysa responded.

"It's all right. She'll be fine," Leo lifted her up before Daisy could.

22

It was hotter than it had been the last week in Yemen, and Daisy could feel herself wilting. She looked over at Effie, who wasn't looking too good. Daisy was going to have to figure out a way to cut this short so that she could get her Director back to the hotel before she passed out. As soon as she thought that, Leo was swapping out her empty water bottle and giving her another one.

"Give it to Effie," she demurred.

"Already gave her one. We're going to have to get her out of the sun soon. Let's get her into the Red Cross tent, then the rest of us can go to the food distribution center."

Daisy nodded. It was a good idea.

"Hey, we're going to make our first stop the Red Cross tent, she called out."

"I'm not sick," Abia said in Arabic. Apparently, the girl had heard the words Red Cross before. "I don't want a shot," her lip began to tremble.

"You're not going to get a shot, I promise you," Daisy said.

Abia struggled to get down out of Leo's arms. "I don't want a shot. Please don't make me." Now she was all-out crying. The tent was a stone's throw away.

"Give her to me, Leo."

"Miss! Don't make me get a shot." Abia held out her arms for Daisy. She couldn't stand it. She took the distressed girl out of Leo's arms. Effie was now next to her.

"Is there something I can do?" she asked in English.

"Abia thinks she's going to get a shot when she goes to the first aid tent. Do me a favor, can you just go there with the camera crew on your own? Maybe take a bit of a break, while I get her settled down?"

"Whatever I can do to help," Effie offered.

"Leo and I will head over to the food distribution area, and that should calm little missy down." Already Abia was not crying as hard now that Daisy had her in her arms, and she was fiddling with Daisy's St. Christopher necklace.

When they started in that direction, Leo asked, "Why are we going there?"

"To discuss the women's committee that I want to start for W.A.N.T. food distribution."

"What will that entail?"

"A whole hell of a lot." Now Abia was playing with Daisy's braid. "I've talked with Maysa and five other women about forming a committee to come up with a way to verify which households are truly run by women. Those households will get extra supplies from our organization. It's going to be massive since there are a million people in the camp. When you consider the fact that two-thirds of them are children or elderly who need care, then you have breadwinners. The estimate is that one in four households are handled by just one woman, therefore we're talking anywhere from twenty to thirty thousand."

"Shit, that's going to be a massive project. Do you put people on the ground?"

"Volunteers. Like I was back in the day. I need to talk to the man handling the food distribution again. He needs to be on-board with our plans, otherwise, this will go sideways fast."

"Understood."

Leo saw the operation up ahead. This was where the few UN Peacekeepers present were deployed. This wasn't where they were needed. He'd already heard where the problems lay, and it wasn't fighting over food in front of everyone as it was being passed out. As a matter of fact, it was amazing how peacefully people lined up to get their rations. But who in the hell had the energy to push and shove?

Granted there was a crowd. Men in rags who had even given up wearing their headgear, except for the grandfathers. The women still wore their scarves, but most were old and faded. He hated to see so many desperate people. What Daisy was doing was nothing short of a miracle.

"Milk. Can I have milk?" Abia asked.

"No, Darling," Daisy said sadly. She looked as heartbroken as the girl.

Leo fished into his backpack and pulled out a butterscotch candy. He'd been saving the package of candies for emergencies, and this qualified as one. He handed it to Abia, and she looked at the wrapped candy curiously.

"Unwrap it for her," Daisy laughed.

Shit, I should have realized that.

As they continued to walk closer to the two men that Daisy needed to talk to, Leo unwrapped the candy and handed it to Abia. The men stood where the water jugs were being filled. There was a lot of activity there. Many hoses came from the truck, with not enough men to man them all. As they got closer, he saw some of the women pointing and smiling at Daisy. She smiled and waved back.

He thought it was odd that they were pointing instead of waving.

When they were just a few yards away, he saw a man, a kid really, holding what looked like a photo in front of his face. He looked at Daisy, then back down at the photo.

Fuck!

He saw the kid reach beneath his long shirt. Leo grabbed Daisy and Abia and twirled them to the ground, making sure that he was between them and the gunman at all times.

"Gun!" Leo roared in Arabic as he heard the distinctive *pop, pop, pop* of a pistol being fired. He felt a sting in his calf.

Abia screamed.

Oh God, is the baby hurt? Is Daisy hurt?

Then he heard something wonderful—Daisy crooning to Abia, calm as could be, trying to soothe the child.

Leo looked up to see what was happening, pissed as hell that he couldn't have smuggled a gun into the country. He saw that one of the men he'd trained had the shooter on the ground with a gun to his head. Why the fuck he hadn't killed him, was beyond Leo's understanding.

Leo looked around the crowd, not wanting to let Daisy and Abia up until he was sure that was the end of the threat. All he saw were shocked faces.

He knelt down and tried to take a look at his two charges, but Abia's arms were wrapped so tightly around Daisy's neck, he couldn't see anything. He tried to move the little girl, but that only made her scream louder.

"It's okay, Baby Girl, I have you," Daisy promised.

"Are you okay, Daisy? Is Abia?"

"I'm fine. I didn't feel anything hit either of us, but you."

"How badly did I hurt you? Can I help you up?"

Before she could answer, he heard the men he'd chosen pushing back a crowd of people who were trying to get to Daisy and the child. He turned around again and saw one of his most senior men coming over to him.

He turned back to Daisy, "Honey, can I help you to sit up?"

"That'd be great."

He wrapped his arm around her back, taking care not to jostle the child in her arms, and got Daisy in a sitting position. "Do you want to stand up?"

Daisy shook her head. "We're good right now."

He turned his attention back to his man.

"What have you got, Abdul?" he asked in Arabic.

"He was acting alone. But, people have been talking about Madame Squires and how she is trying to elevate women. They are not happy. He is deranged and must be punished. I do not know how safe she is."

Leo spared a glance over his shoulder at Daisy. Her already-pale skin looked positively translucent.

"Thanks, Abdul. He's going to be handled by the Amen police?"

Abdul nodded. Despite everything that had happened to him these last few years, he still had his pride. He had served on the police force for many years, but when his leg was shattered in a bombing, he was let go. Eventually, he and his family, including his mother and father, ended up here.

Abdul crouched down to look at Daisy. "You are doing good work here, Madame. I am sorry that some of my countrymen are taking offense. With progress comes pain, and you are their focus. Unfortunately, you will always be the face of your organization."

"Abia," a woman cried from the crowd. "Let me see my baby." Maysa made her way to the edge of people before one of Abdul's men stopped her. Daisy tried to push herself off the ground while holding the little girl but it was impossible.

"Stay seated," Leo growled at her.

"Abdul, that's Abia's mother, let her get by."

Abdul made a hand gesture and nodded to one of his men who let Maysa go, and she came running toward them. She was immediately kneeling in front of Daisy and Abia. "My baby."

Even though Abia's sobs had somewhat abated, as soon as she saw her mother, they kicked back up into full gear. "Is she hurt?" Maysa asked.

"She fell down when the shooting started, but Daisy cushioned her fall. She'll be bruised." Leo didn't go into any more details than that.

"All right, all right. Thank you for saving her. I'm taking her home now."

All the while, Leo could hear her crooning in much the same way Daisy had done. Then he noticed that while Abia hung over her mother's shoulder, she was licking at her piece of candy. The little rascal was doing just fine.

———

DAISY CONTINUED to sit in the dirt, her mind whirling over what Abdul had said. Abia had almost died because of her. What was she doing? Stroking her own ego? Feeling like Mother Theresa out here tending to the people so she could feel good about herself, when really she was bringing danger to their door?

She struggled to get up.

"Honey, let me help you."

She smiled gratefully up at him. When he bent down, she noticed the blood on his ripped jeans and the blood on his calf. "Leo, you've been shot!"

Once again she scrambled to get up on her own power, even though she felt a couple of significant bruises starting to form. Leo practically lifted her onto her feet.

"Don't do that. We need to get you to the aid station! How bad is it?"

"On a scale of one to ten of gunshot wounds, it's a two."

"That's not funny."

"Wasn't meant to be." He put his arm around her waist and walked slowly toward the aid station. She thought he must be really hurt if he was walking this slowly.

"Lean on me, Daisy. I know I hit you pretty hard to get

you on the ground. How are you feeling on a scale of one to ten?"

"I haven't been shot!" Up ahead she saw Effie rushing toward her, along with the two cameramen. She tried to pull away from Leo to get to her friend, then almost stumbled. Her hip was really bruised.

"Daisy!" Effie called out. Daisy waited for her to get closer, then the woman enveloped her in a big hug. "I just heard you were shot at. Why?"

"It's a long story. We have to get Leo into the aid station. He's bleeding—he *was* shot."

Effie looked from Daisy to Leo, then back to Daisy. "I don't know, girl, you look like the one who could use the first aid station. He's the one walking upright, not you."

Leo put his arm around her waist again and continued to guide her toward the first aid tent. She tried to shrug him off. "I'm all right, it's you I'm worried about."

"Every time you push at me, my leg hurts more."

She stopped short and looked up at him. "Oh, Leo, I'm so sorry." Then she saw the twinkle in his eyes. "You are such a...such a...a man!"

His lips twitched. "I'll buy that." He hugged her closer and continued to the aid tent. Her mind was swirling with the idea that she was the reason somebody had almost killed Abia today. Yeah, people had been angry with W.A.N.T. before. They even had a security firm on retainer, and they handled the letters that came in from the crazies, but to be *shot* at?

She hadn't even noticed they'd arrived until they hit the stifling heat and medicinal smells of the enclosed tent.

"He's been shot," Effie told one of the aid workers.

Before the nurse was allowed to look at Leo's leg, he

insisted that Daisy be looked at. "Wait a minute, what about Abia? She should be here," she protested.

"You protected her fall, and if she needs care, her mother will bring her here," Leo soothed. Soon she was behind a very tiny screen, pulling down her pants and showing them what was already the start of a massive bruise on her hip. They got out a one-time instant use cold pack and placed it on her bruise, taping it in place.

"Any place else that's hurting?" the nurse asked.

Daisy hesitated.

"Answer the question," Leo said from the other side of the screen.

"My shoulder hurts. I wrenched it in the fall."

When the nurse tried to lift it above her head, or to the right, she groaned in pain. "You're going to need to wear a sling for a few days so the movement is limited and it has time to heal."

"Now can you look at the man with the gunshot wound?" she said sarcastically.

The nurse chuckled. "I think he'll allow it now."

23

LEO LEFT DOUG'S ROOM, PISSED OFF. HE'D HAD NO IDEA that Daisy had received death threats before as the Executive Director of W.A.N.T. Why in the hell was she gallivanting across Yemen without a security detail? Oh yeah, because according to Doug, she refused to allow the expense.

He banged on her hotel door. "Let me in."

"Hold onto your britches."

If he wasn't in such a surly mood, she'd make him smile.

This time the door wasn't flung open—instead, it was slowly opened by someone who looked freshly showered, tired and sad, and hurting. He looked behind her and saw clothes strewn about and her backpack partially packed.

"You're leaving?"

"Yep."

"Were you going to tell me?"

"Of course I was. What kind of question is that? Come in and sit down on one of my many different seating options." She tilted her head toward the bed.

Leo closed the hotel room door and took note of the fact she even had the window open, letting in the hot air from outside. "That kind of defeats the purpose of the fan," he said.

"It'll get my hair dried faster."

As soon as he saw her try to fold one of her skirts one-handed, he gently pushed her out of the way. "Let me."

"I can fold my own clothes," she protested.

"It's painful to watch. I can do it faster. This way you have time to explain why you're leaving all of a sudden. Don't bother lying to me; this *is* suddenly because Doug doesn't even know about it yet."

She slowly lowered herself to the bed with a wince. He wondered if she had been icing her hip.

"I was going to tell the team after I told you. Obviously, I'm putting everybody at risk here, and I can't stand that thought. I'm going home so I can keep people safe." He saw the anguish in her beautiful gray eyes.

"I applaud your thought process, but this is rather abrupt. Don't you want to say good-bye to the people at the camp?"

Leo watched helplessly as her eyes filled with tears. "I can't risk it. Don't you realize that with my need to glorify myself I'm essentially the same as my father? I'm putting my own ego above the real needs of the people I say I care about."

He threw down the shirt he was folding and crouched down, grimacing in pain. Then he went to his knees instead. "You've done nothing self-aggrandizing. Everything you've done has been to try to help from a humble and honorable point of view. You have always, and I mean always, thought of everybody before yourself. If you ever thought that something you were doing would put people in harm's way, you would do exactly what you're doing now. Leaving. All I'm asking is, is if you want to say good-bye. I can make sure it's safe."

"You can't, Leo. Look what happened today." Her lip trembled but she firmed it up, then stood up, and walked around him. "By the way, no more crying in hotel rooms for this woman."

He chuckled.

"Okay, no crying. No visiting. What do you want to do?"

"I've done it. I've booked my flight. I'll tell my team that I'm leaving, and now we can talk."

Leo stood up. He didn't like the sound of this at all.

She walked toward him then turned around with her back to him. "I can't reach this with my arm in a sling. Can you take off my necklace?"

"Sure." He took off the St. Christopher necklace and tried to hand it to her.

"No, you keep it. I want you to give it to Abia. I'll have you record a video of me on your phone for her."

"Jesus, Daisy, are you sure you want to do it this way?"

"Positive."

"And me? Do I get a video kiss-off too?"

Her mouth fell open. "That's not what you want, is it?"

"No way, not this time. You tell me what you're doing. Tell me what you want. I keep walking out on the ledge, now it's your turn."

She tried to lift both hands up to touch his chest and gasped in pain.

"Without hurting yourself. That's the caveat—tell me what you want without hurting yourself."

"Maybe I'm leaving you before you can leave me."

"Daisy—"

"No. I got you shot. How could you want to stay with me?"

"We've been over this, and you know I'm not going anywhere. I promised. Now tell me what you really want."

He looked into her eyes and finally saw her take down the walls. "I want to spend time with you back in the States. A lot of time. But I don't know how. I don't even know where you live."

"I know where you live, your headquarters are in D.C., and coincidentally I live in Virginia Beach."

Her eyes got huge. "Really?"

"You really want to spend a lot of time with me when we're back in the States? No more blowing off my calls and texts?"

"I was told by a very domineering man that there were new rules that stated I had to return the texts and answer the calls. I agreed to those terms, don't you remember?" Her smile was pure sin.

"I vaguely remember. The problem is, you were naked at the time, so my memory is addled." He traced the line of her jaw, and she stretched so that he was soon touching her cheek.

"My plane doesn't leave for five hours." Her invitation was obvious.

"Then you just have time to go talk to your team and take a real nap. You need to rest, Daisy. Please say you're not traveling coach."

"Of course I am."

"Not when you're injured."

"I refuse to spend money willy-nilly."

"We'll see about that."

Leo pulled out his cell phone and tapped out Doug Prentiss' number. He explained the situation. Doug promised to pull the other members of the team together for a meeting before Daisy left for the airport. He also said he would get Daisy upgraded to business class.

"I can't believe you just did that."

"Believe it," Leo said with a fierce grin. He went over to the house phone and called down for ice, and almost a repeat of the food he'd ordered a few days before. "But bring the ice as soon as you can. Thank you."

"Who said you could come in and take over my life?" Daisy was smiling so Leo knew he didn't have to worry.

"Never would I try to take over your life. Share it? Yes. How does that sound?" he asked softly.

He saw her throat moving but no words came out.

"What, Honey?" he asked as he went closer to her and gently put his arms around her. He tilted her chin up so she was looking at him.

"It sounds scary-wonderful."

"Which part more? Scary or wonderful?"

"I'm pretty sure wonderful, with scary sprinkles on top." But there were no tears, just glittery determination in her eyes.

24

LEO HAD CALLED DAISY EVERY DAY WHEN HE WAS STILL IN Yemen, and by some strange miracle, she answered each and every one of his calls. He sure as hell wished he could go straight to D.C. and spend time with her, but duty literally called. He'd had all the playtime he'd put in for, and had to show up at Little Creek. Max was not going to be happy to find out he'd been shot while on leave.

He'd called and left a message on Max's phone so that he'd have more than a minute to digest the news before showing up in his office on Monday.

"Come in." Max's voice sounded ominous.

Leo went into the small office and found Max and Kane waiting for him. Max was glowering and if Leo had to guess, Kane was smothering a bit of a smile.

"I want to hear every little detail of how in the hell it came about that you spent your leave in Yemen of all fucking places. What's more, how in the hell did you end up saving Dr. Ethan Squires' daughter's life? Would you mind telling me this? Because this picture is not in focus for me, and I don't like it when things aren't in focus."

"I told you, Max—" Kane started

"Shut it, McNamara, I want to hear it from the horse's mouth. Now tell me."

"Maybe he should sit down, seeing as how he was shot in the leg and all," Kane said.

Yep, Kane was enjoying the hell out of this.

"If he were gut shot, I'd think about letting him sit down. *Think* about it. Now, in nice, small-syllable words, explain yourself, Perez."

"There's a humanitarian crisis in Yemen. I went there to help."

"Humanitarian is not a small word," Kane said.

"Shut up, Kane," Max growled.

"What made you decide they needed your help?" Max demanded to know.

Leo hated this. He didn't know what answer Max wanted; did he need him to give him cover for the brass, or did he want the truth?

"I want the truth," Max shot out.

Great, now my boss can read my mind.

"I got to know Daisy while we were in Afghanistan. I followed her to Yemen. I offered my skills as a security consultant for the internally displaced person camp in Aden, it has over a million people."

"I'm aware," Max nodded.

"Daisy was there trying to figure out how her Women's Charity could be of benefit, and she had come up with a very needed and ingenious way to help."

"Go on."

"Unfortunately, there were some men in Yemen who were taking offense and felt like she was trying to elevate women, when all she was doing was giving them a fighting chance in the camp."

"That still doesn't explain how you got shot."

"Apparently, with all the talk going on some dipshit got it in his head that Daisy needed to be killed. I saw him in the crowd and got Daisy and the kid to the ground before he could shoot her. I just took a slight graze."

Max's lip twitched. "Now you can sit down."

"I told you another one would fall on a mission," Kane said.

"What the hell is up with that?" Max groaned. "Seriously, no more women on missions. This is getting to be ridiculous. So, what are the next steps?"

Kane snorted. "Max, this isn't a deployment."

"Bullshit. He wants her, he goes after her. Therefore there are next steps involved. You've followed her to Yemen. You've gotten shot saving her life. Are you going to close this deal, or what?"

Leo's eyes widened—was this really Max Hogan asking him this question?

Max must have seen his incredulity. "Look, Leo, I've already seen it before when one of you has your attention focused elsewhere. It is bad for my team. So, are you cutting her loose, or sealing the deal?"

"Hopefully sealing the deal, but it's going to take some time. I've yet to really go on a date with her."

"Room service?" Kane asked.

Leo glared at the man.

"Go see the doctor and find out when you're ready to train with us again. In the meantime, you're going to help me with some administrative work, and I get to go play on the jungle gym."

Max picked up a six-inch stack of files from his desk and handed it to Leo.

He finally smiled. "Welcome back."

At six-thirty Daisy texted Leo.

What are you doing?

Paperwork. What are you doing?

Wondering what time you get off work, and whether I can interest you in seafood?

Daisy, what are you talking about?

I'm down the street at Waterman's Surfside Grille.

She giggled, imagining the look on Leo's face when he realized she was here in Virginia Beach.

I can be there in twenty minutes, fifteen if I make all the lights.

See you soon.

She put her smartphone down on the table and nodded to the hovering waiter. "I'll take a bottle of sparkling water and put in an order of oysters and calamari."

Daisy nudged up the strap of her sundress that kept wanting to fall down. It was a beautiful day looking out over the boardwalk at the water. Daisy could barely keep herself calm at the idea of her first real date with Leo Perez. When the waiter poured her glass of water, she drank half of the glass immediately, anything to soothe her frazzled nerves.

This is going to work, right? I haven't been imagining things, have I?

She reached up to touch her St. Christopher's medal, but it was gone. It wasn't in her purse or around her neck. Too bad she couldn't go back to that nun and ask for another one. But she wasn't traveling now, was she? Or was she?

She imagined what Abia was doing right now. She

knew that the drawing pads and colored pencils that she'd sent to the children hadn't arrived yet. She had desperately wanted to send an entire toy store but instead kept herself focused on the things that would really matter.

She took another sip of her water.

"Daisy."

His voice almost caused her to drop her water glass. She gazed up and he looked so much better than she remembered. Was it his eyes? Had she ever seen such warm eyes? He stood there beside her, not touching, not saying another thing, just watching her.

"Excuse me, sir." The waiter put the plate of calamari down on the table. "Would you like to have a seat, sir?" he asked.

Leo looked at the waiter and gave a wry laugh. "Sure." He sat down opposite Daisy. The waiter poured him a glass of sparkling water. "Your menu is right there, I'll be back to take your orders in a minute or two."

Leo gave her a slow, sensual smile. "What brings you to Virginia Beach?"

"A man." Daisy smiled back. "I answer the phone when he calls and I return his texts."

"Wow, that sounds serious," Leo said with a grin as he grabbed a piece of calamari.

"So serious that *I* followed *him* this time. I've got a reservation at the Hilton in town."

"Cancel it."

Daisy felt herself go all gooey inside.

She asked "What?" just so he could do the commanding voice again.

"I said cancel it, Daisy, you're staying with me."

"Okay. So what kind of home do you live in? Typical bachelor pad?"

"Mirrors on the ceiling and a waterbed. You're going to love it."

She crinkled her nose. He motioned for her to pick up her menu.

IT STILL BLEW him away that Daisy was here, in his house. It had taken a little persuading for her to leave the rental car at the restaurant and transfer the luggage to his truck so he could drive her to his townhome. He'd finally gotten her to admit that it kind of hurt to drive with both hands on the steering wheel because her shoulder still wasn't healed.

"You sure do travel light. When I tell my sisters' husbands that it's one suitcase and a laptop bag, they're going to want to marry you."

"How many of your sisters are married?" Daisy asked as she preceded him up the steps to the front door.

"All three of them. So are my three brothers. I'm the only unmarried one left."

Daisy stopped on the top stair. "How many nieces and nephews do you have?"

"Fourteen and two more on the way."

"Holy smokes! No wonder you did so well with the kids in Aden."

"Come on, move your tush, we can talk inside."

Daisy stepped up onto the porch. Leo punched in the security code and unlocked the door and had her go in first. He closed the door, then reset the alarm. He saw Daisy peer curiously at his alarm system. He gave an inward sigh. He'd bet his bottom dollar that she didn't have an alarm system. Another thing he needed to put on his to-do list.

"So why was the big-bad SEAL doing paperwork?" Daisy asked.

"Come in and get settled on the couch and I'll bring you something to drink. What would you like?"

"Just water. But tell me why you're doing paperwork," she called after him as he walked over to the refrigerator in the kitchen.

Leo pulled two bottles of water out of the fridge and gave one to Daisy. "This week, no training for me until the leg heals up a little more, so in the meantime, I'm going to be handling a lot of my lieutenant's paperwork. He might have been mad to begin with, but after this, I'll have totally scored points with the man."

"He's mad about how you spent your vacation?" She opened up the bottle and took a sip, then looked up at him. "But why would he be angry? You were helping at the camp, how could he object to that?"

"It wasn't the camp, it was more about you," Leo explained as he sat down next to her on the couch.

"Why me?"

"He realizes just how special you had become to me in Afghanistan and he wasn't really happy about it. Max isn't thrilled with us getting involved with civilians during missions. As a matter of fact, it's been pissing him off."

"Wait a moment. That means that this has happened before, maybe more than once."

Leo grinned. "Yep. This would be the fourth time. Well, fifth time if we count Zed, and he might be Night Storm, but he was working for another lieutenant when he found Marcia, so that doesn't count."

"Huh?"

"Long story. Suffice it to say that yeah, we go on missions but there are some lucky times where we find special women and work damn hard at making sure they stay with us."

"You're losing me, Handsome. But right now I could use a welcome to Virginia Beach kiss."

He set down her cases by the hall table, then picked her up. "I think I can do a little better than that, Baby. Wanna see my bedroom?"

"Be careful of your leg!"

Leo laughed. It was the best he'd felt since the last time he'd seen her. "My leg is fine, Daisy." He walked down the hallway to his bedroom and placed her on his mint green and gray duvet cover.

"You really *do* make your bed," she said as she sat in the middle of it.

"I wouldn't lie. I'm not going to lie about this either; you look beautiful in my bed."

Her smile was incandescent. He flipped on the light on his nightstand so he could admire her even more. "Do you think we know how to do this in a real bedroom, or are we only good at this in a hotel?"

"That's a good question, Ms. Squires. It deserves a good deal of research. Do you know what else needs to be investigated?"

She shook her head, which only made her glossy brown hair shimmer all the more. "What?" Her voice was hoarse.

"This strap keeps falling down your shoulder. I think it's time to get you out of this dress."

"The zipper is in the back," she whispered.

He bent low for a kiss. As soon as their lips met, it was

electric. He gathered her into his arms, spearing his fingers into her silky chestnut locks while his other hand had the pleasure of unzipping her dress. All he felt was the satiny softness of her back. Good God, she wasn't wearing a bra. He pressed her back down onto the bed, his lips never leaving hers.

She pushed at him. "Get this dress off me," she complained.

He huffed out a laugh. "I'm trying to."

"Try harder."

Leo pulled the front of her dress off her chest and arms and let it pool to her waist. Daisy was still talking, but he couldn't understand her. She was breathtaking. Then he remembered.

"How's your hip?"

She didn't immediately answer, so he pulled the dress all the way off her and threw it to the floor. He hissed out a breath when he saw the purple-and-green bruise as big as his hand that covered her left hip. "God, Baby, that has to hurt."

"Not as much as a gunshot wound," she scoffed. "What hurts more is that you're not naked yet."

"I don't think making love is such a good idea right now."

Did I just say that?

"I can't believe you just said that. Damn right we're going to make love. You're in the military. Do your duty. I flew in from Washington D.C. for you. I order you to make love to me."

Leo laughed. "You're a nut."

"A very needy nut. Seriously, get out of your clothes and come closer. I need you."

He took another look at her hip. They were going to

have to go about this very carefully. There was no way in hell he was going to cause her any pain.

"Leo?" her voice was soft. "Please?"

Aw, shit.

He sat down on the bed and traced a finger along her jaw, and then his thumb brushed her bottom lip.

"We do this my way, okay? It would kill me if I hurt you tonight."

"You won't. I trust you."

"My way. Do you promise?"

She nodded.

25

Being made love to by Leo Perez was like being caught up in a summer rainstorm. You were going to come away wet and with rainbows in your eyes.

Now that he was naked, he had her caught up in his arms, careful to not touch her bruise. Instead, he concentrated on every other part of her body. His hands were decadent. They weren't soft, they were work-roughened, and felt so good as they glided over her skin. Every place he touched, sparks fired.

Whenever she tried to move or adjust her position, he would remind her that this was 'his way'. Who was she to disagree?

When he kissed the back of her knee and then licked it, she thought she would shoot through the ceiling. Who knew there were so many nerve endings there? Then when she tried to reach up, he told her no.

"That hurts your shoulder. Put your hand here, and keep it there."

Bossy much?

She kept her hand by her waist, and it did feel better

on her shoulder, but she could still touch him with her other hand, and she was going to enjoy herself. Daisy was addicted to running her fingers through Leo's chest hair. When she felt his fingers delve between her legs, she raked one fingernail against his nipple and he groaned.

"You're going to be the death of me."

How can he talk? I'm going to explode.

She was lost in a world of sensation. She was floating. That was when she realized he was moving her. She was at the edge of the bed, her legs dangling on either side of Leo, who was kneeling on the floor.

She looked over her tummy at him and he had a rakish grin on his face.

"My way."

"Paybacks are a bitch, remember that, Mr. Perez." When did her voice get that breathy?

The feel of his laughter wafted over her sex, just as his tongue started a sensual seduction. Daisy couldn't do anything but feel as first one finger, then another entered her already-swollen tissues. A bubble of feeling started to swell in her chest. It was as if he wasn't just capturing her passion, he was taking control of her heart, her emotions...

"Stop!"

Leo lifted his head immediately.

"Make love to me. You make me feel so much, Leo. With everything that's going on inside me, I just need us to be together. Now."

He stood up and looked deeply into her eyes. His smile was so loving. Another thing that made her heart swell.

He stood at the end of the bed, his erection rising thick and straight and it was all for her. She reached for him.

"Keep your hand down, Daisy," he reminded her.

His hands smoothed down both of her thighs, then he lifted up her legs and positioned them around his waist.

Oh, this will work. This will absolutely work.

In one slow thrust, he possessed her, and just like that, she felt her body start to edge toward freefall. Daisy started trembling at the feel of him as he pushed high and up, causing even more tingling pulses to drive her hotter and higher.

She watched him closely, making sure that he was with her. Was he feeling what she was? Was his heart swelling? Was Leo feeling more than physical passion?

"Daisy." His smile caused her to gasp.

Again he plunged upwards, taking her to unknown heights, but always, his eyes were locked on hers, watching, waiting.

She clasped her legs around his waist even tighter, never wanting to let go, always wanting to be connected to this man. She needed him like rainbows needed sun and rain. He was hers.

"Don't leave me, Leo."

"I'm not. I promise. I'm not."

She clutched him tighter. Her legs, her sheath, her hands gripped his forearms. She needed to know he was real, that he was hers.

"You're killing me, Daisy," he gasped. "Come for me."

"Not without you," she cried out. She couldn't explain it, but they had to be together in this always.

Always.

Together.

Tears dripped down her temples.

He moved his hand and his thumb brushed her clit,

circling it. She shattered, shouting his name. Begging him to come with her.

"I'm here, Daisy. Always."

———

SOMETHING WAS TICKLING HER NECK.

Daisy brushed at it with her fingers, trying to make it go away, but it stayed. Again, she felt something around her neck. It seemed familiar, but not really. She looked over her shoulder and found Leo lying on his side, one arm curled around her, sound asleep. But as soon as she lifted up to leave the bed, his eyes popped open.

"Where are you going?"

"Bathroom."

"S'okay. Come back soon. Like having you in my arms."

She hurried to the connecting bathroom, shut the door, and turned on the light. She had to blink a couple of times to adjust her eyes, then she went over to the mirror to see what was around her neck.

It was a St. Christopher's necklace. But it wasn't hers. It had a different gold chain and a different medal. But that's what it was. She held onto the medal, letting her hand warm it. She breathed deep, wet gulps of air. Leo had done this. He had gotten her a new necklace.

Who else would think to do this?

She looked at herself in the mirror.

"I'm so scared, but it doesn't matter, because I love him so much," she whispered to her image. "I'm happier to be in love and to tell him I love him, than scared if he rejects me."

She grabbed for some toilet paper to wipe away a

couple of tears and blow her nose. *Look at me, being all emotionally mature.* She continued to smile in the mirror, wiping up tears and staring at her new necklace.

She only jumped a little at the soft knock on the door.

"You okay in there?"

"Yeah, why?"

"Honey, you've been in there over twenty minutes mumbling to yourself."

Daisy laughed and opened up the door. There stood her man in all of his confused naked glory.

"I talk to myself sometimes."

He nodded solemnly. "I'm catching on."

"You gave me this necklace. You had it waiting here for me." She clasped it in her hand like she was afraid it would disappear.

"Actually, I told my mom exactly what I needed and she FaceTimed me so I could choose it. It was here waiting for me when I got home."

"You...you...I can't believe you did this for me. It's so damned perfect. *You're* so damned perfect." She wrapped her arms around his waist and nestled her head against his chest.

"I'm just glad you like it, now come back to bed."

She shook her head. "Need to tell you something first." She took a deep breath. "I've been afraid that you would go away."

He kissed the top of her head. "I've noticed. But I'm not. I'm here for the long haul, if you'll allow it."

Her head shot up. If she were taller, it would have bonked his chin. "You're thinking long-term?"

He cupped her cheeks. "Daisy, I love you. I want to be in your life forever."

Her eyes heated as tears threatened. It took her a

moment for her to find her voice. "I love you too, Leo. I really, truly do. I don't ever want you to leave my life."

His lips hovered over hers. "That'll do."

"I'M NOT SURE ABOUT THIS," Daisy said for the umpteenth time.

"It's fine."

"Your lieutenant is mad at me." Another thing she had repeated for the fortieth time. He glanced over and saw her fiddling with her new necklace as she watched the beautiful scenery. The drive to Kane's lake house was gorgeous, just like his house was. Leo wanted to invite Daisy to his mom's for Sunday dinner with the family but figured she'd have a heart attack. He'd been lamenting about that at work and Kane came up with the idea of her meeting the team first as her first baby step to meeting the family. Hence, a party at Kane's house.

"No, Max is not mad at *you*. He *was* mad at me, but I finished all of his paperwork and even got some of his spreadsheets done. He is purring like a lion cub. So I'm now off the hook."

"You do spreadsheets? I didn't know that was in SEAL training."

"You learn what you can to help out."

He turned down an almost-hidden driveway, and then Kane's house came into view. "You've got to be kidding me. This is one of your teammates' houses? How cool is that? It's gorgeous."

He looked again at the contemporary wood architecture that seemed to blend with the outdoors and had to agree with her. There were only four vehicles in the driveway, so they were second to arrive.

Great.

He'd wanted to ease her into things.

"I thought you said there were going to be ten to twenty people, where is everyone?"

"We got here a bit early. I wanted you to get a chance to meet A.J. before everyone else arrived."

"That's nice of you. Thanks for stopping off at the store before we left so I could get some things to take to the party."

Leo snorted. "You didn't get 'some' things. You bought up half of the grocery store."

"I did not, that would have been rude."

He parked his truck, then laughed at her when it took the both of them to bring all the stuff up to the house.

Kane opened the door. "What'd you do, buy up half the grocery store?"

"We went a little overboard," Leo said. "Now take the stuff from Daisy."

"This is perfect," A.J. said when they got to the kitchen. "Put the veggie tray over here, and I've got a bowl for the Greek salad."

"And for being an ass, you don't get any of the brownies," Leo said as he put the treats down on the dessert table.

"Daisy, this is Kane McNamara and this is his much better half, A.J. Lancaster."

"Hi, I'm so excited to meet all of you. A.J., you're going to have to tell me what it's like to produce all of those fun shows. Something tells me it's a lot like herding cats."

"Sometimes even herding large cats," A.J. laughed as she unwrapped the cellophane from the veggie platter.

Leo followed Kane to the grill where Raiden was getting the coals just right. "How's the leg doing?" Raiden asked. "Ready to have your ass kicked on the obstacle course on Monday?"

"I'm in an excellent mood, thank you very much." Leo knew his grin could be seen from the moon, but he didn't care. Daisy had said she'd loved him last night. His life was damn near perfect. Now he'd have to get a ring on her finger.

"Did you see that?" Raiden asked Kane.

"Yep, I did. Don't let him man the grill, he'll burn down my house."

"What are you two talking about?"

"You just went into outer space, obviously thinking about Daisy. I was asking you a question and you didn't even hear me, man." Raiden chuckled.

Leo looked over at Kane for confirmation, but Kane was too busy laughing to nod his head. "You've got it bad, Perez. Has she met the family?"

"She has to go home tomorrow afternoon. No time for a Perez family dinner. But we are going to drop by and meet Mom. Otherwise, I'd get my ass handed to me by my mother."

Zed walked out onto the patio. It had been over a year since Leo remembered seeing his teammate looking so healthy.

"Where's Lulu?" Kane wanted to know.

"Inside with Marcia. I don't think the ladies are going to let her out of their sight any time soon. Met your woman, Leo. Lulu went to her like she was a kid magnet. Says a lot about her. What's the scoop on her?"

"First, tell me about you," Leo asked. "Has the doc cleared you to come back to the team?"

"My doctor has. I have an appointment with the team doctor on Monday. Gentlemen," Zed's grin was huge, "I believe I will be back."

Kane slapped the big man on the back.

Raiden shook his hand.

Leo bumped fists with him.

Considering the fact that they had almost lost Zed, this was really good news.

"So tell me the scoop on Daisy. I like her," Zed said.

"He is all dreamy about her. He'll be in the middle of a conversation with us and lose track because he's thinking about her."

"Ah, God, he's thinking about marriage," Zed said knowingly.

It was hell when your friends knew you so well.

"So what if I am? Seems to me it's worked out all right for you."

"If you find the right woman, I highly recommend it." Zed paused. "Have you?"

"One hundred percent."

26

"I had a great time last night," Daisy said as she pulled her clothes out of his dryer.

"So did I." Leo's hands snuck around her waist and nuzzled her neck. "Are you sure you can't extend your stay one more day? We could spend it in bed…"

"Don't make me drop my clean clothes," she admonished.

He bit her earlobe. When her hands released the clothes, he caught them.

"You're hell on my concentration, Leo."

"Right back at you."

He carried the clothes into his bedroom and she following him. He set them down next to her suitcase and they both started folding them in silence.

She didn't want to leave, either. This had been the best week of her entire life.

"Daisy, maybe I could come and visit you next weekend?"

She dropped whatever it was she was folding.

"I would love that. Can you?"

"We're less than four hours away from one another. I don't see why I can't come up on Friday night and leave on Sunday."

"You don't mind?"

"I told you, always and forever. That includes a four-hour drive," he grinned.

She launched herself at him and he hugged her close. She tipped up her chin, her eyes glowing with another idea. "I could fly down here and maybe telecommute a couple of days and then have the evenings free and then the weekend."

"That would work. Why don't you leave all of your clothes here?"

She loved that. She loved that a lot. "Can't. These aren't clothes I would choose to leave long-term. That would be a whole different set of clothes. Those would be the long-term, man-of-my-life clothes," she teased.

He pulled her into his arms, his lips a mere breath away from hers. "I love you, Daisy Squires." Her heart melted. She believed him.

"I love you too, Leo. With everything in me. You are the best man I have ever known. I just hope I can be good enough for you."

He squeezed her tighter and kissed her. It was electric; he touched every part of her body, bringing her to life. She wound her arms around his neck, trying to get closer. He groaned. The world shimmered and swirled with unimaginably bright colors. He finally released her. "Dammit, we don't have time for more."

She rested her head on his chest. They didn't. Daisy so wanted to meet the woman who raised this impressive man. The woman who had helped him give her this beautiful St. Christopher medal.

"Go get me a glass of water, I'll finish packing."

"You're thirsty? Juice, maybe?"

"I just need you away from me for sixty seconds so I can finish this in peace, otherwise I'm going to pin you to this bed." Her body was achy and greedy.

"I'm going, I'm going," he laughed.

She folded her clothes and packed them into her suitcase at record speed. She was zipping up her suitcase when he came back with some tomato juice. "You need your strength."

"To meet your mother?" she raised her eyebrow.

"To replenish all the vitamins and nutrients you lost last night."

She giggled and drank down her juice.

GLORIA PEREZ WAS EVEN SMALLER than Daisy was. *Imagine that. And she gave birth to seven children, one as big as Leo? Amazing.* They were sitting in her kitchen as she was doling out the blackberry cobbler that she had made.

"This is for tonight's dessert, but since you can't make it for tonight's dinner, you get it now." Gloria smiled.

"Where's mine, Mama?" Leo griped.

"There's a pudding cup in the fridge that you can have." She waved to the fridge, not even looking at her youngest son. "You'll have cobbler after dinner like the rest of the family. Daisy gets hers now."

Daisy took a bite and moaned. "This is delicious."

"It is my mother's recipe. She used lime juice."

"I don't know what she did, but you could sell it to restaurants." She took another big scoop.

"Would you like some ice cream?" Gloria asked.

"No," Daisy answered. "I don't want anything that would dilute the taste of this."

"I've researched your charity. I can't believe all the things it has accomplished. I've already made a donation."

Daisy sputtered and grabbed her napkin.

"You didn't have to do that, Mrs. Perez."

"I told you to call me Gloria. And yes, I did. I think this is my new favorite charity, after St. Jude's of course. Those girls you saved in Africa. It made me cry. All the good work you do. My Leo told me what you're trying to accomplish for all of those women in Yemen. I understand. My husband died many years ago. It is difficult for a woman to raise her family on her own even here in the United States. I can't imagine what it would be like under those circumstances in Yemen. You are to be commended."

Daisy ducked her head and took another bite of the dessert.

"She doesn't take compliments well, does she, *mijo*?"

"No, she doesn't."

"How is your father?" Gloria asked.

Daisy didn't know what to say, she had only talked to him once since she'd been back in the states. "Fine."

"That's another thing that impressed me, that you went to Afghanistan to help your father. That was wonderful."

"Gloria, you're getting the wrong impression of me. I'm not that great. It was my brothers who did all the work. I just was over there to talk to the embassy because I knew how to do that. My brothers were the real heroes."

"And she's modest." Gloria beamed at Leo.

"What was it like raising so many children?" Daisy

asked Gloria. "Especially Leo. He must have been a handful."

"He was. Out of all my children, Leo was always getting into the most mischief. I was so sad when he decided to join the military. Sad and scared. I wanted him to stay close by me, like the others. But he wanted to see the world and fly those planes. I thought that was as bad as it could get. Then he changed from being a Navy pilot to special forces, and he gave me all of my white hair."

Daisy looked at the four strands of gray in Gloria's fabulous black hair that was so like her son's.

"His job is scary, but he does it well." The fact that her father was alive was a testament to that.

"I still wish he could become a local police officer like his big brother Martin, or a firefighter like his brother Felipe."

"It sounds like all of your sons believe in serving others."

"Just like their father. He was a Marine."

"I didn't know that."

Gloria nodded solemnly. "They are all good men like their father. I am blessed." She looked down at Daisy's chest. "Do you like your necklace?"

"Yes. I was missing my medal. A nun had given it to me years ago when I was in Guatemala. I felt lost without it."

"My son, he thinks of everything."

"Okay, time to go," Leo interjected.

"He does not like it when I say nice things about him," Gloria laughed.

"Some time we'll have to get together, just the two of us," Daisy whispered.

"That is a very good idea. Maybe next time, you can come over for our Sunday family dinner."

"I would love to."

Leo hustled Daisy out of the house and got her into the truck. "My mother loves you," he grinned.

"She probably loves all the women you bring home."

He gave her a confused look. "What are you talking about? You're the only woman I've ever had my mom meet."

It was as if the ground fell out beneath her. "Ever?"

He pulled her close, his hand wrapped around her nape so that their foreheads touched.

"Daisy, you're it. Forever. Always."

"Yes," she murmured. "Forever. Always."

EPILOGUE

Four Months Later, St. Regis Hotel

DAISY LEFT THE PODIUM TO THUNDEROUS APPLAUSE. DAISY took one last look at the screen behind her. The final picture still up was of Abia wrapped in her mother's arms, a stunning smile on her face as she held up one of her drawings. Hardly noticeable was the St. Christopher's medal around her neck.

When the lights weren't shining in her eyes anymore Daisy noticed that people were still standing up and clapping. Her cheeks burned. It was ridiculous. She walked down the steps and headed back to the large round table that held people she would never have expected to be dining together.

Leo held out her chair for her, and the applause didn't stop until she sat down.

"You knocked them dead," he whispered in her ear.

"If I had done that, they wouldn't be standing," she griped. "Make them stop."

Alistair, who was on the other side of her, laughed. "No can do, Daisy, you're the woman of the night."

She took a moment to look around the ballroom and saw that people were finally sitting back down. *Thank the Lord.*

"You did good, Sis." Jim was seated across from her, his pregnant wife next to him.

"Darling, I'm so proud of you," her mother said.

"You have raised an amazing daughter." Gloria Perez smiled at Alice Barrett.

"She ended up raising herself."

"Heck of a speech." Martin Perez grinned at her.

"Hear, hear." His wife gave her a warm smile.

"I didn't do anything, it was the people of W.A.N.T. I just got some donations and moved chess pieces around the board."

"And she really believes that," Leo said with a laugh. "It's crazy."

"Daisy is the most impressive woman I've ever known. She is the Maker of Miracles," Ethan Squires said from the other side of Leo.

"I'll second that." Alistair stood up and raised his glass of champagne.

Daisy felt heat flooding her cheeks. Her dad mouthed the words 'I love you.'

'I love you, too,' she mouthed back.

Everybody around the table stood up and raised their glasses.

"To the Maker of Miracles," they toasted.

She reached out and grabbed Leo's hand and he squeezed it tight.

"You're my miracle," he whispered in her ear.

SOMETHING WAS TICKLING HER NECK. Her necklace felt funny. Daisy brushed at it with her fingers. The bed was sublime here in the hotel, but nothing felt better than waking up curled next to Leo. She tugged at her necklace again as she looked over her shoulder and saw Leo staring at her.

"What?" she asked sleepily.

"Nothing, just enjoying the view."

She knew damn well she must look a fright with her dolled-up hair a mess and some of her make-up still on from the night before.

"Don't go second-guessing yourself, young lady, you look gorgeous."

Daisy smiled. The only reason she felt beautiful was because of this man. She tugged at her necklace again; it felt wrong.

"Dammit. I think I broke my necklace."

She sat up in bed, trying to get a look at her medal in the dawn light of the hotel room. Then she realized two things were hanging from the necklace.

"Leo, turn on the light."

He obliged.

Daisy held up the necklace and her heart stopped. A diamond ring, set in platinum, with emeralds on either side was hanging off her necklace. She stared at it, stunned. She couldn't look away. It was the most beautiful thing she had ever seen.

"Say something," Leo coaxed.

She continued to stare. This was it. This was her forever. All of a sudden the ring blurred.

"Ah, Honey, you're crying."

"I want to marry you so bad. I want to have babies with you. Seven, just like your Mama. I want to live with you all the time, no more telecommuting. Can we have that?" She didn't look away from the ring. As she waited for his answer, she couldn't breathe.

"I want that too, Daisy. I don't know about seven."

She jerked her head to glare at him. "Seven," she said vehemently.

"Okay, seven," he gave her a lopsided grin.

"You're my forever," she breathed.

He cupped her face, his lips scant inches from hers. "And you're my always."

I HOPE you enjoyed *Her Sensual Protector*. To stay up to date, get the latest Caitlyn Factor or to discuss the book click here to join my reader group.

ABOUT THE AUTHOR

Caitlyn O'Leary is a USA Bestselling Author, #1 Amazon Bestselling Author and a Golden Quill Recipient from Book Viral in 2015. Hampered with a mild form of dyslexia she began memorizing books at an early age until her grandmother, the English teacher, took the time to teach her to read -- then she never stopped. She began re-writing alternate endings for her Trixie Belden books into happily-ever-afters with Trixie's platonic friend Jim. When she was home with pneumonia at twelve, she read the entire set of World Book Encyclopedias -- a little more challenging to end those happily.

Caitlyn loves writing about Alpha males with strong heroines who keep the men on their toes. There is plenty of action, suspense and humor in her books. She is never shy about tackling some of today's tough and relevant issues.

In addition to being an award-winning author of romantic suspense novels, she is a devoted aunt, an avid reader, a former corporate executive for a Fortune 100 company, and totally in love with her husband of soon-to-be twenty years.

She recently moved back home to the Pacific Northwest from Southern California. She is so happy to see the seasons again; rain, rain and more rain. She has a large fan group on Facebook and through her e-mail list. Caitlyn is known for telling her "Caitlyn Factors", where she relates her little and big life's screw-ups. The list is long. She loves hearing and connecting with her fans on a daily basis.

Keep up with Caitlyn O'Leary:

Website: www.caitlynoleary.com
FB Reader Group: http://bit.ly/2NUZVjF
Email: caitlyn@caitlynoleary.com
Newsletter: http://bit.ly/1WIhRup

facebook.com/Caitlyn-OLeary-Author-638771522866740

twitter.com/CaitlynOLearyNA

instagram.com/caitlynoleary_author

amazon.com/author/caitlynoleary

bookbub.com/authors/caitlyn-o-leary

goodreads.com/CaitlynOLeary

pinterest.com/caitlynoleary35

ALSO BY CAITLYN O'LEARY

Her Steadfast Hero (Book #1)

Her Devoted Hero (Book #2)

Her Passionate Hero (Book #3)

Her Wicked Hero (Book #4)

Her Guarded Hero (Book #5)

Her Captivated Hero (Book #6)

Her Honorable Hero (Book #7)

Her Loving Hero (Book #8)

THE FOUND SERIES

Revealed (Book #1)

Forsaken (Book #2)

Healed (Book #3)

SHADOWS ALLIANCE SERIES

Declan

Made in the USA
Monee, IL
21 January 2022

89519802R00142